Lee William's Quest

THE SEVENTH CHILD SERIES

JOY PENNOCK GAGE

A Land of Heart's Desire
Book 1

Lee William's Quest
Book 2

A Waiting Legacy
Book 3

Lee William's Quest

Joy Pennock Gage

Harold Shaw Publishers
Wheaton, Illinois

Grateful acknowledgment is made to James W. Elliott, author of *Transport to Disaster* (New York: Holt, Rinehart, and Winston, 1962) for the *Sultana* notice used on page 85 of this book.

ISBN 0-87788-487-0

Cover design by Ron Kadrmas

Cover illustration © 1991 by Kevin Beilfuss

Library of Congress Cataloging-in-Publication Data

Gage, Joy P.
    Lee William's quest / Joy Pennock Gage.
        p.   cm. — (The seventh child series / Joy Pennock Gage ; bk. 2)
    ISBN 0-87788-487-0
    1. United states—History—Civil War, 1861-1865—Fiction.
  I. Title. II. Series: Gage, Joy P. Seventh child series ; bk. 2.
  PS3557.A329L4   1991
  813'.54—dc20   91-7754
                                      CIP

---

00 99 98 97 96 95 94 93 92 91
10 9 8 7 6 5 4 3 2 1

In memory
Dustin Bishop Jackson
July 9—September 25, 1984

CONTENTS

CHAPTER ONE

Lee William's Decision

September, 1863

As the first rays of morning light broke over the horizon, Lee William Chidester led his mother's mules along the edge of the cornfield. The brutes followed him single file, plodding slowly under the weight of their burden. Lee William had come to his mama's place long before dawn and loaded the mules with everything that Mama could spare from her root cellar and from the corncrib. Now, at daybreak, he headed toward the cave on Logan Bennett's farm to hide the provisions.

Just yesterday, Lee William had moved what could be spared from his own cellar to the Bennett cave. Logan himself had suggested it and had taken Lee William to the "secret" cave.

Lee William breathed deeply of the September morning air and ran his fingers through his dark brown hair. *Likely Logan never would've taken me to that cave if it hadn't been for Quantrill's gang scattering ever'where,* he thought. The Chidesters had known Logan and Cora Bennett for nine

1

years—ever since Lee William's father, William John had loaded the family into a wagon and moved to Dogwood Creek from Indiana. But in all that time, none of the Chidesters had known about the cave on the lower end of Logan's property.

Since Lee William's father died, he had often turned to Logan Bennett for advice and the older man had taken a special interest in all the Chidester family. Logan had cautioned Lee William that some of Quantrill's gang had been sighted over the county line. He conjectured that if they found their way to Dogwood Creek they would plunder every root cellar and every corncrib they could find. Lee William had listened to his neighbor's advice and, with Logan's help, had moved everything that could be spared.

It had been a somber endeavor for both men, because neither Lee William nor Logan liked to think that the troubles of the rest of the country had finally come to Dogwood Creek.

Coming to the end of the field, Lee William led the mules into the woods where the Bennett property began. There was no path, and he had to pick his way carefully to avoid tangling the mules in the underbrush. He wondered what his papa would say if he were still alive—about the events of the past several years and about the decision Lee William had made last night.

Abraham Lincoln had been president for over two years and had spent the whole time trying to fight a war that began with his election. Hardly anyone in Missouri had voted for the gangly lawyer, and for a time it had appeared that Missouri would join the southern states that had hailed his election by seceding from the Union.

The governor, Claiborn Jackson, sympathized with the newly formed southern Confederacy and led the movement for Missouri's secession. He welcomed the stronghold of the rebel army in the southern part of the state after Confederate general Sterling Price won the battle at Wilson's Creek. Together, the governor and the general optimistically declared Missouri a seceded state.

But Missouri did not choose the way of secession. Instead, she sent her men to march in Mr. Lincoln's army, making her loyalty to the Union official, although hardly unanimous.

In truth, it was neither Union nor Confederacy that concerned most Missourians. Like Lee William's late father, they just wanted to be left alone.

Had Lee William's family lived anywhere else in the state of Missouri, he would have been concerned from the day the rebellion broke out. But Dogwood Creek had proven to be a safe place during Kansas' long bloody struggle for statehood. By the time she was admitted as a free state there wasn't much left of the Union, and that bothered Lee William, but he had to admit that his papa had been right about one thing: the border war had never affected the remote community of Dogwood Creek.

Unconsciously, Lee William slumped his six-foot-four frame as he recalled the past summer when William Clarke Quantrill had ripped through Lawrence, Kansas, killing half the town. Until yesterday, he had continued to believe that Dogwood Creek was safe from Quantrill's gang of bushwhackers. Now, he could only reassure himself that, if Logan was right, the gang members would not present a real danger to the people of the community. They would likely lay low and, under cover of darkness, plunder what food they could find.

Seeing the tree that marked the entrance of Bennett's cave, Lee William told himself once more that he had been right to take Logan's suggestion. There were other dangers to be considered in addition to Quantrill's men. Likely Dogwood Creek could be invaded by foraging troops from the regular army as they scoured the hills for food or animals. For a long time, Lee William had assumed that they were safely removed from the path of the army. But now—well he wasn't so sure. Already General Grant's men had come within a half day's ride of the creek—to Potosi it was—to confiscate mules for his army.

For Lee William, one event stood out above all others, convincing him that Dogwood Creek had been caught in the conflict. When the conscription men came to the creek one day last month, he knew that his family no longer lived in the last safe place in Missouri. He knew there was no such place.

Lee William remembered his mother's contempt for the event. "It seems mighty peculiar," she had declared angrily, "that there's not a preacher nor a teacher ever found this creek since William John died. But the conscription officers found it ready enough. They come galloping through here, demanding three-hundred dollars or off to the army you go."

They had talked about it once—away from his wife Lucy and the children. They had thought to try to raise the money but it would mean losing the farm for certain. And they were reluctant to make that choice.

"Would be a pity, Mama," Lee William had said, "to lose ever'thing you and Papa worked so hard for." And she had responded, "The real pity would be to give up the dream, Son.

4

And I reckon you've worked as hard as anybody for that." It always came back to Little John, who was not quite five. He was Lee William and Lucy's seventh child and only surviving son. They dreamed of leaving a farm to him one day when he had grown.

Lee William had struggled with his decision for weeks, wondering how he could do right by his family and his country all at the same time. Reluctant to leave Lucy and their children, yet reluctant to give up the dream of owning the farm, he had brooded over what to do. But last night he had made up his mind. He would go to fight in Mr. Lincoln's army.

Afterward, he had gone to his mama's cabin and told her of his decision. "I can't think of my children growing up in a wild lawless place if there is any way to stop it, Mama. The way I figure it, the only way to stop it is to keep the Union. I've told Lucy already . . . I've got to go, Mama."

She had peered deep into his eyes and with carefully measured words said to him, "Lucy and I'll manage, Son. You do what you have to do." Her words fell like a blessing on his ears and a great weight melted away. Whether right or wrong in his cause, he felt relieved of the indecision that had plagued him for so long.

He told her about the cave then. He felt sure his mama didn't really believe that Quantrill's gang would ever come to Dogwood Creek. She showed no real concern, but neither did she protest. "If it makes you feel better about us, then do it, Son," she had said.

Coming to the cave, Lee William tied the mules beneath the tree by the entrance. Unlike other caves, Bennett's "secret" cave looked rather like an abandoned well. Its mouth was an irregular circle about six feet in diameter. Bennett had left a ladder in place yesterday after cautioning Lee William to throw it down to the floor of the cave once MaryAnn's provisions were laid in. "No sense in inviting entrance should someone happen on the cave," he warned.

Lee William made his way down, carrying his lantern in one hand and holding the rungs of the ladder with the other. After setting the lantern on a limestone shelf, he hurried back up to unload the animals. A dozen trips later he hoisted the last sack of corn on his shoulder and descended carefully into the dimly lit cave. *It's a mite safer than a root cellar, I reckon,* Lee William thought, *but it's a good thing that Logan will be here to fetch for Mama and Lucy when they need it.*

Looking around the well-stocked cave, he whispered a prayer of thanks to the Almighty that his family had ample provisions. Then, satisfied that he had done all he could, he started up the ladder.

With one foot just reaching to the lowest rung, he stopped suddenly, startled by a noise coming from behind him in the cave.

CHAPTER TWO

Compatriot or Traitor?

───────── ❧ ─────────

Lee William stepped away from the ladder, immediately turning toward the noise he had heard. *Maybe a rock falling,* he thought, *a rock dislodged by the sacks and bushels.* He stood still, listening intently. A moment later, he heard something move.

He held the lantern high above his head, directing its light into the outer corners of the cavern. A startled face peered out from behind the provisions Logan had carried in yesterday.

For a moment Lee William stared. Then he approached the wall of grainsacks. He held the lantern up again.

"Come out of there, Jim Smith!" he commanded. "What on earth are you doing here?"

A young man came out slowly, his hands extended to show he was unarmed. Jim Smith had shared their table for their first months on Dogwood Creek before he left to open up Kansas for slavery. Lee William had never anticipated seeing him again.

"Things getting too hot for you on the border, Smith?"

"I'm glad to see you, Mr. Chidester," the young man admitted. "I been needin' to talk to somebody but I been skeered to show my face. I 'membered this cave from when we lived here and figured I'd be safe. . . . I thought I was the only one that knew about the cave. When I climbed down last night and found somebody'd been here hidin' plunder, I reckoned the Feds had been here for sure. I hid good when I heard you comin' this mornin'. But not good enough, I reckon." Jim's boyish face held a mixture of panic and relief and shame.

Lee William shook his head in disbelief. "Logan Bennett and I hid these provisions here yesterday, hoping for a safe place. Bennett was sure no one else knew of this cave."

"I don't reckon anybody else knows," the young man reassured him. "I just happened onto it once and I kep' it to myself—my own secret. But I won't bother you none, Mr. Chidester. I'm just lookin' fer a place to hide."

For a moment Lee William said nothing. Remembering their first winter on Dogwood Creek, which had been spent in the Smith's abandoned cabin, Lee William reasoned that he had to give Jim a chance to tell his story.

"Come on out here where I can see you," he said roughly. Jim obeyed. "Now, suppose you tell me what you're doing back on Dogwood Creek. I thought you'd all gone to fight the cause of the bushwhackers."

To Lee William's amazement, young Smith covered his eyes with his arm and began to sob. "Mr. Chidester, I be tellin' you the truth. They ain't nothing but a bunch of outlaws. Ma and Pa and me went to the border 'cause we figured Kansas oughta be open to slavers. We went fightin' for the south. But now—"

"Now what? Go on, boy."

"I cain't take no more. The whole border's awash with blood, and that's the God's truth." Smith gulped and got enough control to keep talking. "It don't matter if it's jayhawkers or bushwhackers, they're all a bunch of killin' outlaws. I was with Quantrill and Anderson when Ewing rounded up all the women—wives, sisters, mamas, even lady friends of Quantrill's leaders—and clapped 'em into jail. Then Bill Anderson's sister died in there when the building collapsed, and Anderson went mad. When Ewing ordered all women and children of the guerrillas to remove from the district, it just stirred up Quantrill. That's when they all decided to go to Lawrence."

"You were with Quantrill's men at Lawrence?"

Smith nodded dejectedly. "It was so bad I just purely had to go behind a tree and puke when it was all over! Quantrill went chargin' into town afore sunup, and first man we saw was sittin' milkin' his cow in his yard. One of the men just shot him dead. Later someone read in the paper that he was a preacher—him what we killed first. We killed half the town, seemed like. But old Jim Lane—the one that Quantrill was really after—he got clean away. He was too smart for Quantrill."

Calmer now, the boy dropped down onto the grainsacks and continued, "And Quantrill didn't lose one man 'cept fer Larkin Skaggs, what used to be a preacher. He wuz too drunk to ride, so we left him behind. I hear tell some Injun shot him and they dragged him through the streets, and folks just ripped him apart.

"We hid out 'til Ewing ordered all the people left on the border to get out. My folks left—hardly had any clothes to wear. They had their old wagon, but they wuz both walkin' so some of the children and old people could ride. Ewing

9

swore nobody'd harm the people who wuz leavin', but he ain't got any control over them jayhawkers. They come right behind the folks who wuz leavin' and robbed 'em and burned their homes. My ma was killed in a skirmish along the way, and I don't know what happened to Pa."

Jim Smith looked at the floor of the cave as he spoke, and Lee William, listening patiently, sat down near him.

"I made up my mind I was leavin', and first chance I got I run away. Quantrill—he'd slit my throat if ever he found me. I figured if I got clear of them I'd join up with the Union army."

"Are you telling me that you're going to fight for abolition now?" Lee William asked in surprise.

"No, sir, Mr. Chidester. I'm goin' to fight for the Union. I reckon I don't feel no different about a man's right to own slaves. But where I was, there warn't nobody who wuz fightin' for other people's rights—they just wanted what wuz right for them. Most of the time that meant stealin' and killin' ever'one who got in their way. I can't never forget I wuz part of that, but I aim to do different. I aim to right some wrong, if I can."

Something about Jim's outpouring struck Lee William as the truth. He sat for a long while, saying nothing. If he could be sure the man could be trusted, he would help him. But he didn't want to expose Lucy and the children, or Mama, or even the Bennetts to this bushwhacker turned Unionist, if it was a guerrilla trick.

"You don't have no reason to trust me," Smith said, as if he knew Lee William's dilemma, "but I be needin' some help. I want to get to the Union headquarters and sign up—if they'll have me."

10

"Well," said Lee William rising, "I'm going now. If I can see my way clear, I'll be back before sundown. If not, you'd best be out of here by this time tomorrow, or Bennett's liable to slit your throat."

Jim nodded and stood at the foot of the ladder to watch Lee William go.

Lee William rode away, filled with new concerns for his family. He left the mules in his mama's barnlot, hung up the halters, and then saddled the old work horse without even going to the house. He rode directly to the Bennett home. The roar of Bennett's hounds brought Logan to the door.

"Better get down, Lee William," he called.

"Can't. But I have something to tell you."

"Somethin' wrong, Lee William?" Logan approached the horse, and the two men spoke in undertones. Lee William quickly recounted his meeting with Smith and asked for advice. "Should I trust him, Logan? He seems bound to join the Union army; I could take him with me when I go. But I don't know how much to trust him. You've known him longer than most—"

Logan scratched at his beard thoughtfully. "Let's go talk with Jim," he suggested finally.

Later, satisfied that Jim Smith could be trusted, they laid out a plan. Smith could lay low for the rest of the day in the Bennett's spare room and get some proper rest. Come night-fall, he and Lee William would leave for the army. They would travel by night until they reached the nearest army head-quarters.

"Be at my mama's barnlot at dusk," Lee William instructed Smith, swinging his tall body up into the saddle. "I'd best go and tell my family I'm leaving."

––––––––

It was still early when Lee William made his reluctant good-byes to Lucy and the girls and Little John. He wanted to be at his mother's place well before Jim Smith arrived there. He wasn't taking any chances.

He walked through his mother's open door calling, "It's me, Mama," and scolding, "You've got to keep this door closed. Pull in the latch string and be a mite more careful."

She looked up at him, surprise registering on her face. Then, as if remembering their conversation about outlaw bushwhackers, she said, "I'll remember."

Lee William stood quietly, twisting his hat between his hands. Before he could speak what was on his mind, his mother asked softly, "You're goin'. You're goin' now. Is that it, Son?"

"Yes, Mama. I'm going. I already said good-bye to Lucy and the children. I just came to tell you."

"You're leavin' tonight yet? Some reason you can't wait 'til mornin'?"

Carefully choosing his words, Lee William explained the situation. He tried to make it sound as natural as milking a cow that a pro slaver would turn Unionist. But MaryAnn would have none of it. She questioned how a slaver would come to fight for the slaves.

Lee William tried to explain. "Remember what Mr. Lincoln says, Mama. It's the Union we're fighting for. Some folks fight because they want to free slaves. Some folks fight because they think the states should stay together. And Jim—well, he wants to fight to right a wrong. I want to help him get that chance."

And with that, Lee William was gone.

———————

That evening, MaryAnn never even lit the lamp. She closed the door, pulled the latch string, and dressed for bed. She lay pondering her great weight of responsibility for Lucy and the children. Could she be as strong as Lee William needed her to be? Would they be safe until he came home?

"Oh God," she prayed, "will he come home? Even before he gets to battle, I reckon he's takin' a mighty big chance sleepin' with Jim Smith nearby. Don't seem possible that a bushwhacker can really turn Unionist. I reckon time will tell. Time will tell."

CHAPTER THREE

Unexpected Help

─────── ❧ ───────

MaryAnn's wondering about Jim Smith lasted only until November when a letter came, saying that Smith had proved himself a loyal Union man and saved Lee William's life in the process.

The letter, which MaryAnn picked up at Carrick's Mill, was addressed to Lucy, and MaryAnn hurried to the hilltop cabin to deliver it. She handed it to Lucy, knowing full well that in a moment her daughter-in-law would hand it back, for the blonde, blue-eyed young woman had never learned to read. Lucy held the letter lightly in her palm, opened it, and handed it to her mother-in-law. Then, motioning for Mary-Ann to join her, she sat at the table and looked up expectantly.

MaryAnn started reading.

My dear wife and children,
I am afraid that I have sad news for you in a way. Young Jim Smith died during our first skirmish with rebel soldiers. But I hope it will cheer you to know that he

*proved his loyalty to the Union in the end. He threw me
to the ground today when we were surprised by rebel
shots. He told me, "You got to be more keerful, Mr.
Chidester." When the skirmish was over, he was dead.
And if he hadn't thrown me down, I'd be gone, too.*

At this MaryAnn paused, and the two women looked at
each other. MaryAnn could see her own pain mirrored in
Lucy's eyes. She breathed a prayer of thanksgiving for her
son's safety. *Now if only we can manage to hold things
together here,* she thought. Already the two women had
discovered that running a farm without a man around was
no easy task.

———

A week later, Lee William's brother, Russell Brean
Chidester, came to Dogwood Creek. Russell's letters from St.
Louis had been scarce over the past months. When he first
left Dogwood Creek, he wrote regularly, especially after his
father died. But since the outbreak of the rebellion, when he
went to work for Mr. Eads, he had written only a few hastily
scrawled notes, saying he had little time except for work.
MaryAnn had not written him that Lee William had gone off
to war for she knew Russell would worry over her. It had not
occurred to her that Lee William might write to Russell
himself.

On the morning that Russell came, he hardly took time to
greet MaryAnn before he scolded her. "Mama, why didn't you
write me that Lee William had gone to the army? I would
have come." Then, tugging at his withered left arm, he
blurted out, "I would have gone in his place if they would take
a man with one good arm." At thirty-five, he stood a few

16

inches shorter than his younger brother. His blue-black eyes and raven hair marked him as his mother's son, and the telltale gesture of pulling at his useless limb signalled his irritation with her.

He looked around the kitchen, taking in the woodbox and the water pail, both of which were full. Then, a bit more gently, he asked, "How have you managed with no man around?"

"Like ever'body else, I reckon. There's hardly any menfolk left 'round these parts. Lee William was here for most of the season. Lucy's pa was here through first plantin', but he's gone to Turkey Holler. He's still cuttin' timber for the boat-yards."

She urged him to sit at the table, then brought coffee and cold biscuits with jam. He drank deeply while explaining that he had received permission to be away from Mr. Eads's boatyard for a time. "I've got to go back before bad weather, Mama, but I had to come see about you and Lucy."

———

For two weeks, from daylight to dark, Russell worked at everything he could find to do. At night, he sat staring into the fire, tugging at his useless arm. He said nothing, but MaryAnn knew that Russell hated being there. He stayed only out of obligation, for the beauty of Dogwood Creek had never captured his heart the way it had hers.

When the first snow clouds appeared and Russell made no mention of returning to St. Louis, MaryAnn questioned him about his plans. He gazed at the fire. "I don't know, Mama. I can't rightly see how I can leave you here with no help."

When MaryAnn protested that she could manage—that Russell shouldn't change his plans on her account—he ig-

17

nored her and went off to bed. They didn't discuss the matter again.

——————

A week later, just before daybreak, a light snow began to fall. Russell hurried to the barn, intent on doing the milking, and feeling agitated over his situation. Coming to the heavy barn door, he set the milk pail on the ground, grabbed the door handle—and paused. There were voices coming from within.

Cautiously, Russell pulled the door open. There before him stood a man, a woman, and three little children. They huddled together, panic written on their faces.

Had it been the man alone, Russell would have ordered him off the premises immediately. But the sight of the children, wide-eyed and trembling, took away his resolve.

The man spoke first. "Please, mister, we mean no harm." He rose and stood in front of his family.

"Where are you from?" Russell questioned.

"Down New Madrid way. The rebels run us out of our homes. Whole town had to leave."

"That's a long way. Is the whole town coming to sleep in my barn?" Russell's tone was harsh.

The man shifted uneasily, and the smallest girl began to cry. The woman quickly shushed her and looked fearfully toward Russell and then toward her husband, as if willing him to speak.

"No, sir," the man replied. Then he cleared his throat and shuffled his feet before continuing, "Most folks gone to Rolla to catch the cars to St. Louis. Hear tell the government may put 'em up."

"You must have passed Rolla coming here. Why aren't you on that train to St. Louis?"

"We not be city folk."

"Well, a man can't always choose where he wants to live—'specially when the whole country's at war," said Russell gruffly.

The man eyed Russell carefully. "We figured to start over again someplace where the rebels ain't likely to come."

"Well, you just may have found the place." Russell spat the words out. "Nobody comes to Dogwood Creek. On the other hand, we don't take kindly to squatters!"

"We don't want to be beholden to no man," the man answered quickly. "But with winter comin' on, we can't camp outside no longer."

Russell surveyed the group. The oldest child, a boy, was about school age. The girls were younger. Too young to be out in the cold he realized. He shrugged. "I'll just do the milking, then I'll take you to the house. We'll see what can be done."

The woman sat back in relief, and the children stared up at Russell. The man said, "Don't want to put your missus out none."

Russell tugged at his limp arm. "Not my missus. Don't have a missus. This is my mama's place, and my brother's. But he's gone to fight with Mr. Lincoln's army."

———

It was snowing again when they left the barn—enough to have covered Russell's earlier tracks completely. He stooped to pick up the middle-sized child even as the man raised his youngest to his shoulders. The children's shoes were worn through.

19

The man followed Russell's gaze. "It's the walkin'," the man apologized. "They had good shoes, but we been a long time on the road. We carried 'em some."

Russell wondered to himself how the man could have carried the children, for he walked with a considerable limp.

As if he could read Russell's thoughts, the man offered an explanation. "Took a rebel bullet at Wilson's Creek," he said.

Russell nodded sympathetically. "Did the rebels take your horses, too?"

"Yep—the good ones. Left some worn-out ones. We had one the first day on the road. Then he plumb gave out. Just laid down and died."

MaryAnn was frying ham and didn't look up when the door opened. "Mama," Russell said, " 'Pears we have company for breakfast. Don't rightly know their names."

"Broom," said the man. "Broom, ma'am. Jacob and Martha. Our young'uns here are Jacob Junior, Jessie May, and Bertha—we call her Bertie."

MaryAnn greeted each of the strangers enthusiastically as they made their way through the kitchen door. Her eyes sparkled as she urged her unexpected guests to gather around the fireplace. Afterward, she returned to the kitchen and sliced off more ham to add to the pan. When it was finished, she made a big pan of gravy. She set out cold cornbread left from last night in case the biscuits didn't go around. And at the last minute she fetched some applesauce from the cellar.

After they had eaten, Jacob Broom wiped his mouth on the back of his sleeve and spoke gratefully, "Thank you, ma'am. We're indebted to you. But we don't want to be beholdin'. P'raps I could do some work fer you in return?" And then, with a look of dejection, he continued, "I'd be obliged iffen you'd let us rest in your barn a few days. Family's plumb tuckered out."

Russell jumped in with a reply before his mother could answer. "You'll not go back to our barn!"

MaryAnn looked up quickly at Russell's hasty words. Embarrassed, she noticed that Jacob Broom looked like a whipped dog.

"But son—" she began. At the same moment Jacob Broom spoke, "We wouldn't be no trouble. I'd be glad to milk or do whatever you need in exchange . . . "

"No, no," said Russell, realizing he was being misunderstood. "No need for that, Broom. I think I know a place you can winter. It's just a timber cutter's cabin, but it's tight and nobody's using it." He turned to his mother. "I'll walk up to Lucy's and see if these folks can use the last cabin her pa built. Then I'll go on up and get a fire going. It ought to be ready by evening, I expect."

MaryAnn was pleased. She spent the morning preparing a supply of food and answering the Brooms' many questions about Dogwood Creek. Russell returned to find her dividing some of her quilts to share with the destitute family.

"Well, the fire's going," Russell reported. "Arial went with me and cleaned out the dust and cobwebs. Lucy sent some canned goods and a couple of spare quilts, too."

After hastily consuming a big dinner, the Brooms set off to their new place, with MaryAnn and Russell walking along. On the way they stopped at Lucy's. The children eyed one another shyly, all except Bertie and Little John who immediately took to one another.

"It'll be right nice to have neighbors so near," volunteered Lucy.

Immediately recognizing her Tennessee speech, Jacob bluntly asked, "Ma'am, what if your pa don't take kindly to folks hidin' out from rebels in his cabin?"

"You'uns have come to a safe place," she insisted. "Not ever'body from Tennessee is a rebel. Lots of folks on Dogwood Creek is hidin' out."

Jacob Broom volunteered to help out in any way he could, in return for all their kindness. To MaryAnn's surprise, Russell replied that he had to return to his job in St. Louis. "I'm leaving first light tomorrow. If I can count on you to help the women, I'd be obliged."

Later, Jacob Broom repeated his promise as he shook hands with MaryAnn and Russell at the door of Jubal Tate's cabin. "I'll watch out fer your family, Mr. Chidester. We're mighty grateful fer a warm place, a safe place."

Russell nodded and said, "Well, Broom, we can't promise you safety, but one thing's for sure. Dogwood Creek is the last place anybody'll come."

CHAPTER FOUR

Russell's Dreams

———————— ❧ ————————

Russell and his mother tramped a short distance through the snow in silence. Then, looking up at her son, MaryAnn spoke.

"Russell," she accused, "you talk like Dogwood Creek is the end of the world!"

"It's a nice enough place, Mama. But it's no place for a woman alone," he replied adamantly.

"You're forgettin', Son. Some women are different. My mama crossed the country in a wagon with no man to help her."

"And you left a perfectly good farm in Indiana. Why don't you go back there to Uncle George?"

"Because, Russell, a body can't up and move right in the middle of a war. And, even if I could, I wouldn't. That Indiana farm would never be mine. William John was right about that. And it would never be Lee William's or Little John's."

Russell grabbed at his useless arm. "Why is it so important to leave a farm to Lee William? Would you leave one to me?"

MaryAnn sighed. "If it was in my power to do so, and if you wanted one, which you don't. You don't understand at all, do you?"

23

"I understand that Pa worked himself to death on this dirt farm, and now you're doing the same."

"And why shouldn't I? Why should I be different from my mama? Life on the frontier's always been hard."

"Is that what you think this is?" Russell's voice rose angrily. "Mama, Dogwood Creek's not the frontier. The frontier's where people go and get ready for the rest of the country to catch up with them. The frontier has already passed you by! Railroads have gone in and you're fifty miles from the nearest one. Roads are in, but you're twenty-five miles from the nearest. There's no doctor. Nobody's interested in schools or churches. Don't you see, Mama? The frontier is stretched clean beyond this godforsaken place. A hundred years from now Dogwood Creek won't be any different, except there won't be anybody left who has ever seen a teacher or a doctor or a preacher."

MaryAnn pondered his outburst for a long while before she answered. "I reckon I never thought of it that way, Son. But don't make no difference. I don't ever want to leave here. I love it here. I love these woods . . . even in winter. I feel peaceful here." Her eyes seemed to plead for understanding, but Russell gave her none.

"Then stay!" he exploded, pulling at his arm. "Stay on this dirt farm if you want. Raise your chickens, keep your cows, grow your garden and enough grain to feed the animals—if the locusts don't get it! But you can't support yourself and the family on land that is five inches deep. It's a godforsaken place and nothing's ever going to change that!"

The louder he yelled, the harder he tugged at his arm. Finally, MaryAnn could stand it no longer. "Stop that!" she demanded, jerking his good hand away from his limp arm. "I don't ever want to see you do that again."

Russell looked at his arm. He grew still. "I'm sorry, Mama. It's a bad habit, I reckon."

"You're always a-doin' that when you're upset . . . 'specially when you're mad at me."

"Oh no, Mama," he said, his anger completely cooled now. "Not you. I do it because I'm mad at myself. I'm mad because I keep thinking I should be somebody I'm not. First off, *I* should be one of your sons that's in the bury ground back in Indiana—they had two good arms. If one of them had lived and I had died, you'd have had a son more to your liking."

MaryAnn turned to him, startled. "Russell—" she began.

But Russell's stream of words continued. "I've started this, let me finish. I should've been more like Lee William . . . loving the land and all. But I'm not. Even with two good arms I'd never be what you wanted me to be." He tugged at the arm, unconsciously. "Whether I'm here milking your cows or in St. Louis working for Mr. Eads, I can't get it out of my head that you're wishing I was somebody different. No matter how hard I work or how much Mr. Eads likes my work, I keep remembering that you would rather I'd be working this farm. But I'm never going to be a farmer, Mama! Mr. Eads is proud of my work—says he's never had a better bookkeeper. I expect to work for him the rest of my life."

MaryAnn looked surprised. "Son, I didn't figure you liked your work in St. Louis that much. You never talk about it."

"You never ask. Seems like if it's not about broken plows or fences that need mending, you don't figure it's worth talking about."

"Is that what you think?" MaryAnn could hardly believe what she was hearing.

"What am I supposed to think? What do you even know about what I do?"

"I know Mr. Eads is buildin' boats for the Union."

"Built, Mama, *built*. And they don't call them boats. They call them ironclads. He built eight of them in one hundred days and had to hire four thousand men to work around the clock. That meant a lot of bookkeeping! It was a very important job, and I was proud to be part of it."

MaryAnn stared at her son. "I can't believe you never told me that."

"You never asked."

They walked in silence for a long while. Then MaryAnn tucked her arm through his useless limb. "I'm sorry, Son. 'Pears we've misunderstood each other a lot. I always wanted to see you do whatever it is you want to do. Uncle George says, 'It's mighty burdensome to try to follow someone else's dream.' I reckon if he was here, he'd tell you to find your own dream, and I say so, too."

"Time enough for that when the rebellion's over. Right now I just have to know you're going to make it through this winter all right."

"Well, now, I thought you had that all arranged," MaryAnn replied. "I reckon those Brooms are the Almighty's provision, for sure."

"Maybe so," said Russell thoughtfully, "but I have another idea."

Coming to the kitchen door, they stomped the snow from their feet and went inside. As they hung their wraps, Russell laid out a plan. He urged MaryAnn to bring Lucy and the children to live with her and let the Brooms use Lucy and

Lee William's cabin. It would bring the neighbors closer and make the work easier on Jacob Broom.

———

Lying in bed that night, MaryAnn wondered why she hadn't thought of Russell's suggestion herself. She resolved to speak with Lucy about it the next morning after Russell left. Then, remembering that it would be Little John's birthday, she said aloud, "I wonder where his papa is. I wonder where Lee William is."

CHAPTER FIVE

Homesick

~~~

Autumn, 1863

Somewhere in the vicinity of the Cumberland Gap, a slow, drizzling rain fell on a camp of Union soldiers.

Private Lee William Chidester sat quietly in the midst of milling men, waiting for the order of the day. He had awakened early—in the middle of a dream about Lucy. During these past few days as his batallion moved through Tennessee, he had thought of little except Lucy, and home.

Along with a few other enlistees from Missouri, Lee William had been assigned to the Third Battalion of the 16th Illinois Cavalry under Major C.H. Beer. Presently Beer was intent on raiding Confederate-held Powell's Valley, where he hoped to collect the food supplies his men needed so badly.

Lee William prayed in the silent shadows of dawn. "Almighty God, take care of Lucy and the children and Mama. You have to care for them—they're all alone with no man to care for them." He paused, wishing he could find the words to speak to God about his own predicament.

His mind whirled with bits and pieces of the past few years—from John Brown's brutal murder of the Kansas family to the vicious slaughter on battlefields in recent months. Among three hundred cavalrymen, he felt alone and deserted. It wasn't just that he missed Lucy and the children. He felt a deeper desolation—a desertion by the One he had always accepted as loving and kind, and protective.

From his earliest memories, Lee William had accepted that God was almighty and that He listened when His children prayed. As a child, he would crawl up on his papa's lap and listen as Papa read from the big Bible. He had readily accepted whatever Papa taught him, for it was never his nature to question those who were supposed to know more than he knew. Certainly he had never before questioned God. *But that's exactly what I'm doing now,* he thought. The idea was new and strangely disturbing.

Questioning God seemed akin to doubting his very existence. And if God was not there, did anything in life really matter? If He was there, where did He fit into this ugly war?

To Lee William's peace-loving mind, it didn't seem that God could be on either side of the issues over which the states were warring. He couldn't believe that God would condone the brutality that had occurred on both sides. After long months of soul-searching on this question, the lack of an answer discouraged him to the point where he thought he'd lose his mind.

He was still deep in thought when the signal for boots and saddle sounded. He had learned quickly that being in the cavalry meant being on the move; he reacted automatically. He saddled his horse, buckled on his saber and revolver, mounted, and fell into line as his company counted off by fours. The bugle sounded the call to move forward.

A bitter cold replaced the rain. The men rode silently all morning, straggling unevenly across the frozen ground. Lee William's mind continued to brood over the haunting questions. In the months since his assignment to Beer's army, he often wondered what his dedication to the Union might cost his family. Mama had given her blessing, had said they would get along, but Lee William couldn't shake the feeling that he had acted impulsively. Many times he wished he had not been so stubborn about the money. Was saving the farm worth leaving Lucy and Mama without a man to care for things? Somehow he could have raised the $300 and stayed home. For an instant, as the wind whipped around him, he wished he could just turn around and ride off in the other direction—all the way back to Dogwood Creek.

As if he could read Lee William's thoughts, the major riding alongside suddenly commanded, "Eyes front, soldier!" Lee William sat up sharply. The company had reached the top of the ridge. An instant later they heard shots.

The major charged ahead to examine the situation. Turning, he yelled, "Company I, march!" Lee William swung around into line with his company. The men drew sabers and revolvers and—yelling at the tops of their lungs—charged into battle.

Lee William clamped his teeth and ignored the sickening feeling in his stomach. He took aim at the line of rebel soldiers. In a few minutes, that line was reduced to a mass of wounded and dying men lying on the frozen ground.

As his company moved forward over the hill, Lee William saw Confederate soldiers breaking rank and running down the hillside into the woods.

"After them!" called the sergeant, and Lee William urged his mount down the hill. Suddenly he found himself face to face with a young rebel soldier. There was no time to take aim, no time to think. He fired; the bullet tore through the rebel's chest, and he dropped. Lee William saw the blood running from the fallen soldier, and he urged his horse further into the woods. There, under the thick cover of trees, he leaned over his horse and wretched.

When he caught up with his company, the battle was over. That night, around their cook fires, they spoke of the day's success. They had driven out the Confederates and had opened Powell's Valley to the Union army. The next day there would surely be food.

But Lee William couldn't think of food. He closed his eyes to sleep and saw only the red blood of the rebel soldier. He wanted to wretch again.

————

Powell's Valley provided even more food than they had hoped for. For weeks Lee William and others of his company guarded those who had been assigned by the quartermaster to foraging detail. As the foragers loaded grain into wagons, Lee William stood guard, eyes alert for the slightest movement. When not on guard duty, he joined small foraging teams as they searched abandoned farms for apples and winter vegetables. Every day they brought in turnips, pumpkins, cabbages, and potatoes. At one deserted homestead, Lee William discovered a smokehouse full of hams. Every night they ate until they were full, and Lee William sent up a prayer that his own farm had not been ransacked and that his mother and wife and children were safe in their homes.

He was often seized with a great longing for Dogwood Creek, and the sight of the abandoned mill where they ground their corn reminded him of Carrick's Mill at home. He comforted himself with the thought that perhaps taking Powell's Valley would be a turning point. *Maybe the war will be over and we can all go home soon.*

At the end of a long day, he tied his horse securely and examined its fetlocks and legs to make sure all the mud from the day's travels had been rubbed off. Then he withdrew from his jacket an extra bunch of hay and held it out to the animal.

He and a fellow-soldier retired to the sleeping area they had prepared. He spread his poncho and then his overcoat over the mattress of pine needles. The two lay down together, having learned that both could be warmer if they shared his friend's overcoat and both of their blankets. Boots, belts, revolvers, sabers, and carbines were removed and left within reach.

The bugle sounded taps and the camp prepared for sleep. Lee William fell asleep at once, but he was awakened during the night by the sound of frozen tree limbs cracking under their weight of ice. Afterwards, he slept fitfully until reveille.

Barely into his boots and preparing to roll his blanket, Lee William was startled by the shout of his captain to turn out. A rebel yell pierced the morning air and a volley of rifleshot followed.

As far as Lee William could see into the woods, there were rebel soldiers. They rushed into camp, yelling and firing. Company I quickly closed ranks and, without time for mounting, returned fire on the advancing rebels.

Though greatly outnumbered, Lee William and his company held their ground all morning. They continued into the afternoon, sometimes advancing, sometimes falling back.

"Where are they coming from?" Lee William shouted once to his sergeant. "They've got us outnumbered bad!" The man shook his head. They were ill-equipped to deal with the waves of advancing rebel soldiers.

Lee William fought near the cannon, giving cover to those manning the great gun. Midafternoon he spied a large group of rebels running for shelter behind a rock wall on the hill. Quickly they poked their guns over the wall. At Lee William's warning, the cannon operators loaded the big gun, pulled the lanyard, and broke through the wall.

This small victory hardly stopped the rebels. Lee William used the last of his cartridges and retreated to reload. Under the trees he found his sergeant, badly wounded.

"Chidester." The man spoke with labored breaths. "How's it goin'?"

"Not good," Lee William had to answer. "We're almost out of ammunition, and they just keep coming. It doesn't look good."

Lee William tried to make the sergeant comfortable, but it was plain to see that the man was dying. Just as he breathed his last, Lee William heard the bugle summon the company to the hill. Coming into position, he saw Major Beer raise a cloth of surrender. A rebel officer rode out and approached them.

"Who is in command?" the rider demanded.

"I am," replied the major.

"I demand your sword!"

"What is your rank?" the major asked. "I will never surrender to my inferior in rank!"

The rebel turned back to his company, and Lee William joined the others in cheering the major. But the cheers died as the rider returned with a colonel. Without further word, the major surrendered his sword.

Lee William's eyes grew misty. They had fought a long day's battle, and they had lost. There was only one more thing he could do for the Union. He snatched the cylinder out of his revolver and hurled it away. Next he removed the slide from his carbine and disposed of it similarly. All around him the other men did likewise. Then they stood defiantly, awaiting the order to throw down their useless firearms.

The Union prisoners were marched to a field and ordered to camp for the night. Cold and hungry, Lee William joined a group of men who were hunched together, talking in low tones about the day's events and what might become of them now.

"They'll be sure to bring us some grub, don't ye think?" one young soldier asked.

Almost as he spoke, a rebel soldier passed by and issued each man a small sack of cornmeal. Turning it over in his hands, Lee William speculated on how to make use of it when he had no kneading pan.

Another soldier stood up. "I reckon this'll have to do," he said and turned over his cap.

Lee William also emptied his meal into his cap, then scooped water from a nearby spring. Using a twig, he mixed the meal to a firm, sticky dough. He spread his dough on a wide, flat stone and set it in front of the fire.

When it had baked on both sides Lee William ate the saltless cake slowly. In spite of his hunger, he found it difficult to swallow. The eating did little to ease his hunger. Mostly it just made him homesick, calling up thoughts of real cornbread warm from Lucy's oven.

He considered his predicament. He was now a prisoner of the rebel army. His future seemed more gloomy than ever. With no horse to care for, he had nothing to do but lie down to sleep, wondering what the morning would bring.

CHAPTER SIX

Andersonville

———— ❧ ————

For four days the prisoners marched in icy cold over the mountains and into Bristol. There they were herded onto cars and jostled to an unknown destination.

On the morning of the ninth day, Lee William felt a sudden lurch and the train ground to a stop. At a guard's order, Lee William vaulted from the car. Outside, he could see that the car had jumped the tracks, and the rebel guards were scurrying around, trying to make the necessary repairs. Others kept a watchful eye on the prisoners.

Lee William stretched his arms up over his head and surveyed the countryside. He overheard the conversation of two guards who were angrily discussing prisoners confined in the second car down the tracks. "I reckon they'd otter hang 'em all—anybody frum Tennessee that'd fight agin the South!"

Something inside Lee William jumped. He looked at the indicated car. Men were hanging out the door, where a guard prevented them from leaving. Lee William inched around his own companions and came to the car full of prisoners from Tennessee.

As soon as the guard turned his back, he sprang into the car. He worked his way into the center and called, "Anybody named Tate in this car?"

The men grew quiet, but no one volunteered any information.

Lee William tried again. "Anybody here kin to Jubal Tate from Little Rock Holler?"

A man stepped forward. "Who be askin'?"

"Lee William Chidester, raised in Indiana and now from Dogwood Creek over in Missouri. My missus is Jubal Tate's daughter. Thought some of you might know him."

The lanky Tennessean before him thrust his hand out. "I be a-knowin' him. I be Lute Tate. Jubal's cousin to my pa. I'm proud to know you. How come you'uns is on this train?"

"Rebels captured us at the gap. We're what's left of Beer's army," Lee William explained.

Immediately several officers from the Tennessee regiment stepped up to see if Lee William knew anything about an exchange of prisoners, but the train jerked forward before he could answer. Lee William moved toward the door. "I've got to get back to my outfit!"

"Jist where do ye think ye're goin', traitor?!" the guard barked at him. And without waiting for a reply, he slammed the door in Lee William's face.

Lute laughed. "It don't matter where you ride. We'll all prob'ly end up longst side each other anyways."

"Where do you think that'll be?" Lee William questioned.

"Don't rightly know. Wherever they keep traitors, I reckon. I heard tell they voted Missouri into the Confederate states, so that makes all Missourians fightin' for the Union traitors, too. 'Course, to us, they be the traitors."

"Voting us in doesn't make us part of the rebel nation," Lee William said angrily. "Fact is, Missourians didn't secede!"

———

Lee William spent only one night on the Tennessee car. Early the next morning, the cars ground to a stop and all the prisoners were ordered off the train. Several hours later, they were deposited in a tented prison camp.

"I reckon this be Belle Island," Lute observed. "Way I heared it, Rebs keep a lot of Union prisoners here."

"How do they survive in this cold with nothing but tents to live in?" Lee William wondered aloud.

"You're in for a little surprise!" a nearby rebel guard said and then laughed.

When Lee William saw his company, he fell into line with them and marched off. Lute called after him, "I'll look you up, Chidester!"

"You'll camp here," the guard ordered harshly, stopping in a large empty spot.

"Where do we get tents?" asked a sergeant.

"Shucks, now," the rebel guard replied. "We're plumb out of tents!" Then he turned on his heel and left.

———

Lee William's company kept a fire going day and night. Lee William practiced moving about close to the fire and never sitting for more than half-hour stretches. He slept lightly at nights, rising often to stomp around. During the long days he spent hours exchanging family tales with Lute Tate.

"Reckon we'll ever git home?" Lute asked one day.

Lee William jumped up. He rubbed his limbs and stomped his feet. " 'Course we will. We'll make it. One thing's for sure—things can't get any worse than this."

————————

In mid-February 1864, Lee William's outfit was ordered to move. Before sunup one morning the outfit fell into line. Lute ran toward the line. Lee William waved his cap at him. Lute stepped up and grabbed his hand.

"Where you goin', Lee?" he asked.

Lee William shook his head. "Don't rightly know."

The two men stared at one another, then embraced. Lute slowly walked back to his own outfit as Lee William marched away to the waiting cars.

On the eighth night of traveling, the train stopped at midnight and the guards ordered the prisoners off. Outside, the air was heavy with the scent of pine trees. Even in the darkness, Lee William could see that they were in the middle of a forest. Before them stretched a road, dimly lit on both sides by piles of burning pitch.

"Follow the road!" the guards ordered. The men moved ahead, silent except for the cadence of five hundred prisoners marching between double lines of armed guards. Lee William guessed they had marched a quarter mile when he saw a great stockade looming before them. In the pitch light he could see logs so massive that the tops were lost in shadows. Lee William wondered how high the stockade might be and whether it was their destination. *Anything's got to be better than the last place,* he thought.

The expected order to halt came from somewhere down the line. The prisoners stood still, waiting for what would come. Two guards removed a bolt from the center of the massive, wooden gates, swung the gates open, and told the prisoners to enter.

As Lee William passed through, a rebel guard curled his lip and spoke directly to him: "Welcome to Andersonville, Yankee!"

Lee William awakened early the next morning, while many of his fellow prisoners were still asleep. Rising stiffly, he moved about to inspect the enclosure. He gave a low whistle and shook his head unbelievingly. There was not a proper shelter in the whole place. His heart sank. He hadn't believed that anything could be worse than Belle Island!

Walking to a corner of the stockade, he paced off a portion of it and estimated that the entire stockade probably enclosed about sixteen acres. The walls were tall, thick pine logs—at least two feet around and about twenty feet high—standing so close together that Lee William could not see anything outside the wall.

Rebel soldiers stood guard on the perches on the top of the wall. One glared at Lee William for a moment. Lee William hesitated, then turned and walked toward the center of the stockade. There he came upon a slim trickle of a creek, which he guessed was the water supply for the whole camp.

From the vicinity of the gate through which he had entered the night before came the unmistakeable rumble of wagon wheels. He watched as the massive doors swung open and a wagon loaded with sacks and vegetables rolled through. *The ration wagon,* he guessed.

His ration proved to be a quart of meal, a small portion of salt beef, and a sweet potato. Lee William took his ration and joined a friend.

"Well, Ben," he said, "looks like that tin pan you made is going to come in mighty handy. Rebs don't seem to have anything that passes for cooking utensils. At least they're not offering any to us."

"Don't pay it no mind, Chidester. We can both use this."

They poured their meal into the pan, saving out a small amount. "I'll see to a fire; you can mix this at the creek," Lee William offered. "And see if you can find a big, flat stone to bake our hoe cakes on." He collected timber scraps from a pile of debris.

While their hoe cakes baked, Lee William browned the leftover handful of meal in the pan and fetched more water from the creek. He brought the water and browned meal to a boil. Satisfied that it had boiled long enough, he handed the pan to Ben. "Rebel coffee," he remarked. "Have a drink."

At midday, guards came and ordered the prisoners to count off into hundreds. The prisoners then separated into groups of twenty-five and began looking for some way to construct a shelter.

Ben and Lee William set out together to build themselves a hut of some kind. "First off, Chidester," Ben suggested, "we gotta find some kind of tools. Might be hard puttin' up a hut without an axe."

An hour later they had located no axe, but had found one small hatchet and two pocket knives among the men in their division. "We're third in line for the hatchet," Ben reported.

Before sundown they were able to chop down some willow branches from the swamp near the creek. They bent these into half circles and jabbed the ends into the ground. The next day they gathered some vines and set to weaving their hut. Soon it began to look like a basket turned upside down.

"Reckon we've got a new thing in baskets, Ben," Lee William said as he surveyed the structure. "I've used bushel baskets or pecks, but this . . . well, I never heard tell of a two-man basket before!" He laughed.

"Just need one thing yet, Chidester," Ben replied. "We got to git some pine needles and thatch the whole thing. That should make it good 'n tight."

———

A day later, their thatching job complete, Lee William and Ben looked at their finished work and around the stockade at the other completed shelters.

"I think the worst is over, Ben," Lee William declared. "At least we all have shelter now."

Ben grinned and quickly agreed. "Them rebel guards is all mighty surprised to see our shelters. Guess they figured we'd all lay down and give up, seein' as how they didn't issue any tools."

"Hey there, Ben," greeted another prisoner from nearby. "I heard what you said. We don't intend to give up for no rebs! Fact is, some of us is figurin' on gettin' out of here. You two interested?"

Ben and Lee William looked at each other. The excitement in Ben's eyes echoed the beating of Lee William's heart. Lee William answered for both of them: "Count us in!"

CHAPTER SEVEN

Not Forsaken Yet

—— ❧ ——

Two days later, Lee William and Ben huddled with the other men and planned their escape. They quickly concluded that the escape could best be carried out by scaling the wall on one side of the stockade where two of the logs were a couple of feet shorter than the rest of the wall. The men spent the remainder of the morning pooling bits and pieces of information.

"I'm sure we went through Macon, Georgia, just before we turned south," volunteered one man. "That means we have to be in the southwest corner of the state."

A second man miraculously produced a map. "Tore it out of a schoolbook," he explained. "I wanted to know where I was. It's kinda worn, but Georgia's all there."

Ben studied the map. "If we are in the southwest corner, then Flint River is not far east of here. Look here!" He pointed to a spot on the map.

Lee William also bent over the map. "And look what else!" he said excitedly. "The Flint River flows right into Appalachicola Bay. We have gunboats there . . . at least we did last time I saw a newspaper!"

"Come on, Chidester," said Pete, a tall New Yorker. "How're we going to get to the Bay?"

Lee William had already thought of that problem. "I figure there's a good chance that the creek running through the stockade empties into the Flint. So once we made it over the wall, we could follow that creek to the river and then raft down."

"So all we have to do is get over the wall," said Pete sarcastically. He sounded so skeptical that Lee William wondered why he had bothered to join them. Before Lee William could speak, the others jumped in, declaring that it could be done. So Lee William held his peace, but later he confessed to Ben that he was uneasy about Pete.

"How's that, Chidester? What do you know about him?" Ben asked.

"Nothing, I guess. Just a feeling," said Lee William. "Forget it."

After the men laid their plans, they set about gathering any strings or cloth they could find to make a rope. Ben, who'd served a stint in the Navy before joining the three-year army, volunteered to make it. Lee William watched the process, frequently helping to stretch and test the weight.

As the two men worked together, Lee William fell silent. Finally Ben asked, "You seem mighty deep, Chidester. Thinkin' 'bout the escape?"

Lee William smiled. "No, Ben, not really. Not this escape anyway. Sitting here in this basket shelter of ours and planning an escape over the wall calls to mind my pa's story of Paul in the Bible and how he escaped over a wall in a basket."

"Never heard that one. Your pa a preacher?"

Lee William shook his head. "Schoolteacher. He died six years ago."

"You a religious man, Chidester?" asked Ben, looking up from his work for a moment.

"A year ago I would have said yes," said Lee William, sitting down. "Now I don't know. I've done a heap of troubling over things."

"I never been religious myself," said Ben, "but my ma prays for me every day. The way I see it, if you're a religious man, Chidester, you better be prayin' for God to help us git out of here."

"My ma's the same . . . she prays a lot. Learned it from my pa, I guess. He used to say to her, 'MaryAnn'—that's Mama— 'the Almighty hasn't forsaken us yet.' He never was one to worry. But he died—" Lee William broke off suddenly, slightly choked, and blinked his eyes.

Ben asked, "Things go hard for you when your pa died?"

"It all started before that," Lee William said truthfully. "But it's a long story."

"I ain't goin' anywhere!" Ben laughed, tugging on the rope. "Leastways not today!"

"Well, I grew up in Indiana, on the farm my grandpa and his grandpa homesteaded. You see, my grandpa had come to America when he was a little boy and settled in Tennessee. There were six of them—his two brothers, his parents, and his grandpa. One day he went hunting with his grandpa and when they came back, they found the house burned and the family massacred by Indians. They left the very next day for Indiana. And there the two of them, a young boy and an old man, homesteaded a farm. That's the farm where I grew up."

"Why'd you leave there?" Ben queried.

"Partly because Pa took it into his head to have a farm of his own, instead of sharing one with Uncle George, and partly because my pa was tired of fighting for free schools in Indiana. One day he just gave up, and the next thing we know we're all moving to Missouri."

"How come Missouri?"

Lee William laughed. "Well, my pa's horse was stolen one day, and he tracked it clean to Dogwood Creek. When he brought the horse home, he was full of plans to move. 'Course I didn't have to go. Lucy and I were married and had one girl. But I jumped at the chance to own my own land. I didn't know that Missouri land was half rocks! And I reckon Ma didn't know it either."

"Your ma didn't want to go?"

"She went easy enough. But when things got rough in Missouri, she took to hating that horse of my pa's that had started the whole thing. The very day she came home from Pa's burying, she sold that horse."

Ben laughed a deep-throated laugh, but Lee William grew quiet again. "My ma . . . she complains some, but she still prays to the Almighty, just like Pa always told her to. Me, I've had a hard time praying ever since the Pottawatomie massacre, when John Brown got so crazy."

"How come?"

"I'd figured God to be on John Brown's side, but then he got so crazy and—"

"You an abolitionist, Chidester?" Ben interrupted.

"Don't rightly know, Ben. None of us liked how Indiana wouldn't allow black people to live there so we didn't mind leaving at all. Then the year we moved, all hell broke loose in Kansas. I thought God must be on the abolitionists' side because I can't believe it's right that any man should own another human being. So, for a time, I called myself an abolitionist."

"Ever go to Kansas?"

"Never. But I followed it all in the papers and made my little speeches every chance I got." Lee William stared at Ben's hands as they worked at the rope. "I wondered about some things they did, even at the beginning . . . like why did the eastern abolitionists send folks out to Kansas with a Bible in one hand and a gun in the other? And preachers! Both sides have preachers, and each said God was on his side. It all got mighty confusing."

"But you figured God was for the abolitionists."

"Yes, at first. But then John Brown massacred that family at Pottawatomie. The way I see it, God couldn't be on the side of anybody who'd split a man's head open with an axe." Lee William fidgeted. "I guess what I'm saying, Ben, is that when I joined the three-year army, it wasn't to fight for abolition. I'm a Union man. I think the only future of this country is in the Union. Now my pa . . . he always figured we could hide out on Dogwood Creek and let the rest of the country solve the problem. And he never questioned where God fit in. Me, I've spent so long trying to figure out God that I've forgotten how to pray."

"You still believe in God?"

"I think so, Ben. But I feel mighty alone. I think I could believe a mite easier if I could understand why God's allowing all this to happen."

Ben dropped the rope in his lap for a moment. "I don't know much about God, Chidester," he began, "but it sounds to me like you're askin' God to do a lot of explainin'. I always

49

thought it was the other way around. I mean, when I do think about God, I get kinda worried that someday God will want me to do some explainin'."

Lee William looked up at Ben with clear eyes for a moment, but a scraping at the door interrupted their conversation. Two fellow prisoners came in with more scraps for the growing rope.

"Just in time!" exclaimed Ben. "I'm almost out. Here, give it a yank. Think it's strong enough to hold a man?"

The men grabbed and pulled. They handed the rope back to Ben, smiling. "Won't keep you from your work," they said, moving to the doorway.

Pausing there, one of the men said, "Last count, fifty promised to make the break. Pete says he ain't goin', though."

Ben shot a glance at Lee William, but his friend was silent, not wanting to betray his uneasiness.

———

In a few days, Ben's rope was thirty feet long. The men agreed to make the break for freedom that night. Lee William found a stout stick, and Ben fastened it to the rope's end.

"That tall feller from the next hut oughta be able to throw it over the wall," said Ben. "If he aims right, the stick'll catch between the tops of the logs and hold the rope for us."

"I'll go find the stones for drawing lots," Lee William volunteered. He spent the afternoon gathering fifty small stones and etching a number onto each. He piled them up, numbers hidden, and late in the afternoon, the men came by to choose the stone that would give them the order of their turn for going over the wall. Finally, there was nothing left to do but wait.

When it was dark, they crept single file to the wall. Lee William watched as the rope was secured. Silently, he counted off the men until he came to his own number: twenty-seven. He held his breath as the first man scaled the wall and slid over the top. When they heard the soft thud of his fall on the other side, they sent the number two man over. Soon fifteen more had gone over the wall.

Ten more, and then me, thought Lee William, his heart thumping against his rib cage.

Suddenly, from the other side of the wall, there came the angry command of a rebel guard.

"Halt! Halt! Halt there, I say!"

"Run!" Lee William whispered loudly. The remaining prisoners fled to their huts. Moments later, Lee William heard shots. He and Ben slid into their basket hut at almost the same moment.

"Chidester!" Ben panted. "The guards opened fire right on the spot where we was standing. One more minute, and we'd all be dead!"

CHAPTER EIGHT

Dark Days

————— ❧ —————

It seemed plain to Lee William that they were stuck at Andersonville stockade until the Union army rescued them—and that could take a long time. As near as he could figure, Andersonville was probably the furthest point from the Union lines. At last report, Sherman, the closest Union force, was at least four hundred miles away in Chattanooga.

The next morning Lee William and Ben discovered what had happened to the men who had climbed over the wall. The rebel guards had been waiting. They had grabbed the escapees silently one by one, until one nearly got away. The seventeen who made it over had been brought back, every one of them in balls and chains. Ben and Lee William speculated that the guards had known about the plan.

Later, Ben brought Lee William news that confirmed their suspicions. "Chidester," he called softly, leaning closer to where Lee William was building the fire, "Pete's been given reg'lar duty in the commissary."

"So that's a traitor's reward, eh Ben?" commented Lee William.

"You were right about him, Chidester."

———————

Two days later Lee William and Ben sat in the doorway of their hut, watching a gang of men who'd been brought in to drive a line of stakes about twenty feet from the stockade wall.

"No-man's land," conjectured Lee William. The workmen began to nail lengths of cloth from one stake to the next.

Ben shook his head. "I guess our big escape idea only made things worse. Sure looks like the rebs are aimin' to keep us away from that wall all right."

When the line was finished, an order was issued: any prisoner crossing the line or even touching it would be fired upon without warning.

Later, near the creek, Ben and Lee William watched as a prisoner walked close to the line. Without warning, a guard fired and the prisoner fell to the ground, dead.

The group of prisoners stood silent for a moment. Finally one man spoke up. "Take a good look at that fancy fence of stakes and cloth. What you're seeing is a dead line—cross it and you're dead."

For days, Lee William brooded over the incident. Ben noticed his long silences and restlessness and finally asked, "Somethin' botherin' you, Chidester?"

"How much can a body take?" Lee William answered. "We got nothing but an upside-down basket on a dirt floor to sleep in, very little to eat, we're hundreds of miles from our lines, and now we've got gun-crazy guards. It's hardly safe to go near the creek. Things couldn't get much worse."

The rains came in March. Day after day, sheets of rain drenched their huts, saturated their worn prison garb, and turned the stockade area into a muddy wallow. With it came a bitter wind, biting the faces and fingers of the prisoners.

And as the skies emptied into the stockade, the Confederates continued to empty their prisons into it. Great loads of prisoners came off railway cars and straggled through the massive gates in groups of 500 or more two or three times each week. They slogged about looking for space to put up shelter. Soon there was nothing left with which to fashion a shelter. But still the cars belched forth new lots of prisoners.

Lee William hid himself in his tent, not so much to escape the rain as to spare himself the agony of having to look at so many men with no escape. Staring at the top of his basket hut, day after day he silently demanded, *Where are you, God Almighty? And whose side are you on anyway?*

By the end of March, over two hundred and fifty men had died of pneumonia, consumption, or dysentery.

With April's milder weather, Lee William began to hope that conditions would improve. He said as much to Ben one morning.

"The sun's mighty welcome, for sure," Ben replied. "But it's too late for lots of 'em. They're carryin' a dozen bodies a day outta here."

While the rains had ended, there was no end to the cars, or the prisoners who flooded in. One morning, late in April, Lee William awoke with the feeling that something extraordinary was going on in camp. Here and there he could hear men stirring and speaking in excited whispers.

Hurrying to the door of his hut, he peered out across the grounds. Where there had been a road the night before, he now saw a sea of prisoners sleeping so close that there was no room for stepping.

He shook Ben awake, and his friend came to the hut door sleepily.

His face awakened with a look of horror. "Looks like the rebs dumped the whole Union army in here! There can't be nobody left out there fightin'!"

"And uniforms!" Lee William gave a low whistle. "There must be twenty carloads of officers."

The two men walked out to a better vantage point.

"One thing's for sure, Chidester. These men are too clean to have seen much fightin'," Ben pointed out.

He spoke softly, but a uniformed officer nearby stirred and sat up, carefully checking around him. His eyes rested on Ben and Lee William. "Tell me men," he said, scrutinizing their ragged apparel, "How long have you been here?"

"Goin' on three months, sir," Ben replied.

"And before that?"

Lee William spoke quickly of Beer's army, Cumberland Gap, and Belle Island.

Ben interrupted him. "Looks like a powerful bunch of you. Where you from?"

The officer nodded. "Two thousand. We've been garrisoned at Plymouth, North Carolina, on the Roanoke River. Rebels arrived a week ago. We held out three days, but, as you can see, they took the garrison."

"You've got a blanket leastways," Ben said.

"They did allow us to keep all our personal effects," the officer replied.

"You're mighty lucky, sir," Ben commented.

"I suppose you could say that. But I can't stop thinking about how I was to start my furlough today. I just got my veteran pay."

Lee William shook his head sympathetically. Then, reaching out his hand, he said, "Good luck, sir."

"Thank you, soldier."

On the way back to their hut, Lee William and Ben compared situations. The new prisoners were able to keep their personal effects: blankets, money, good uniforms, cooking utensils. But there was no room for even one more tent in the stockade, and almost no wood. And all would receive the same small ration.

Back in his basket hut, while Ben was off getting water from the creek, Lee William pondered over the fact that out of so many prisoners, so few of them had shelter. Yet he was one who did. He wanted to make little of it, but something nagged at him. There was a picture he couldn't get out of his mind: he was standing with all the family in the Smith's cabin on Dogwood Creek, a week after their long journey to Missouri. Mama had expected they'd have to live with strangers and was so pleased that they had a deserted place to use while they built their own. She'd quoted some Scripture that was unfamiliar to him: "The Lord God went before, seeking out a place to pitch your tents . . . " She'd been convinced that God had prepared that place for them. Now he wondered if the same were true of him. And he wondered why he found no comfort in the possibility. Hut or no, he still felt abandoned.

Ben took longer than usual at the creek. And when he came in, he had news. "Seems as if the new prisoners have decided to spread the wealth. Think we can squeeze one more man in here, Chidester? That officer we talked to this morning said it would be worth ten U.S. dollars to us if we kin squeeze him in. All the new prisoners are talkin' to the men with huts, tryin' to bargain for a place to sleep."

"If we sleep spooner fashion, we could take two," Lee William volunteered.

"At ten dollars each? Chidester, you're a real business man!"

"I wasn't really thinking about the money, Ben. I was thinking that it would give two more men some place to sleep."

"I know," said Ben. "I'll go tell the officer right away."

But by the time Ben had reached the man, the officer had made a deal with Pete for less money and plenty of room.

"I feel mighty uneasy about a man who just got his veteran pay laying down in the same tent with a traitor like Pete," said Lee William.

" 'Zactly what I thought. I warned him and he thanked me, but he wasn't a bit worried . . . figured he could take care of himself."

———

The next morning, Ben and Lee William volunteered for corpse detail. As unpleasant as it was to help carry out the dead bodies of their fellow-prisoners, the duty offered them a chance to gather firewood from outside the stockade wall.

Near the gate, Ben spotted the body of the officer they had spoken with. He was stripped of his fancy uniform; his throat had been slit from ear to ear.

"Chidester!" Ben exclaimed.

Lee William took one look and turned away, ill.

Later, their job completed, Ben and Lee William returned to their hut with an armload of scraps for the cook fire. All day long Lee William brooded over the turn of events. He kept to himself, only once voicing his thoughts to Ben.

"Seems like we've got enough trouble with the rebels and this cattle pen they call a prison. It doesn't seem right we should have to worry about prisoners fighting other prisoners!"

"Well, at least you and me got nothing anybody'd want," said Ben. "Look at us! Hardly 'nough uniform to cover us decent anymore. They'll likely not bother us if we keep our distance."

"You sound just like my pa!" Lee William spoke with sudden anger. "Not every problem can be solved by staying away from it!"

"What? You figurin' on takin' on Pete and his gang?"

"No, I'm not. But it seems like with all the officers dumped in here, some of them could take charge of things. Can't see why we have to put up with a bunch of outlaws in Union uniforms. They're stealing blankets and rations and utensils from the sick. Seems to me we're all still in Mr. Lincoln's army, even if we're prisoners. And some of the officers ought to get a little control in here before things get any worse."

Within a week, Lee William observed that the officers had posted guards around their own group, though they made no effort to set up order within the camp as a whole. Little by little, the rest of the men followed the officers' example. Able-bodied men took turns standing guard around each mess-group. And there was peace around the camp . . . for a little while.

CHAPTER NINE

Soul-Singing

———————— ∽ ————————

Week after week, the prisoner count increased, and the daily rations decreased. By the end of July, there were over 30,000 men confined to the stockade and each man was receiving only a small amount of meal—no meat and no vegetables.

The sky that had so recently left them awash in a great muddy bog now became a burning expanse of brass, blistering the loose skin on the near-skeletons of Mr. Lincoln's army. Six wagons carried out the dead each day.

Lee William learned to move to and from the creek without ever looking directly at another prisoner. Eyes cast down, he hurried through his daily errand. When he returned, Ben invariably asked, "See anybody, Chidester?" and Lee William repeatedly answered, "No one, Ben." And then he would sit in the hut the rest of the day, making no sound other than the quiet, persistent cough that had recently come upon him. He no longer demanded answers from his father's God; he no longer offered even a whimper of request to the God who had seemingly abandoned him for good.

On the morning of July 28, as Lee William went to the creek to fetch water, he heard a rifleshot. Looking toward the cloth and stake line, he saw a prisoner fall. He shuddered, turned his eyes back to the ground, and stooped to fill his pan. Shaken, he forgot his determination to avoid the eyes of his fellow-prisoners. As he stood, he found himself gazing into the face of another prisoner.

"I beg your pardon, soldier," said the man. "I'm C.J. Barnes. You look mighty troubled. Any way I can help you?"

"No offense," said Lee William, making a hopeless gesture with his hands. "No one can help me except Sherman himself, and I reckon he's too far away."

Barnes studied Lee William for a moment. "You're forgetting someone else. Are you a praying man, soldier?"

"Praying man? I used to be," Lee William answered slowly. "But I found out that God is even further away than Sherman. I don't put much stock in Him anymore." There was no anger in his tone, only despair.

"A lot of us are going through bad times here," Barnes said softly. "But some of us have been meeting for singing and preaching over by the east wall. Maybe you'd like to join us?"

"How long has that been going on?" Lee William asked, his surprise shaking off some of the stupor he'd been dwelling in for weeks. "Where'd you find a preacher?"

"Been meeting regular for a while now, but this is a big place. You probably wouldn't have heard about it unless your sleeping space is near where we meet. And the preacher? That's me." C.J. Barnes smiled. "Why not come out tonight? You might find some comfort."

"Nothing will comfort me again unless it's being home with my Lucy and our children." Lee William felt ashamed of the tears that were rising. He looked away, staring at the dead line once more. "I used to be a religious man, Barnes. I purely did want to do what God said was right. I wanted to be on His side."

"But not anymore?"

"Fact is, Mister, I can't figure out what side God is on." Doubt passed like a shadow over Lee William's face. Then abruptly, for he did not want to talk with Barnes any longer, he said, "Thanks for the invite. I'll remember where it is if I decide to give it a try." With that, he turned on his heel and strode away.

When Lee William got inside the familiar basket hut, Ben asked him, "See anybody, Chidester?"

"A preacher," said Lee William. "A preacher right here in Andersonville stockade."

The singing had already begun when Lee William crept into the outer edge of a semi-circle of fellow prisoners. He coughed now and then but listened closely.

> *When I can read my title clear*
> *to mansions in the skies,*
> *I'll bid farewell to ev'ry fear*
> *and wipe my weeping eyes . . .*
> *I'm goin' home to die no more,*
> *to die no more,*
> *I'm goin' home to die no more.*

A great longing swept over him. He realized with some surprise that it was not a longing for Lucy and Dogwood Creek. It was a longing for *true home*. For the first time in years he saw clearly that his deepest longing was to make his peace with Almighty God. He wiped the corner of his eyes with the back of his hand, sighed deeply, and moved a bit closer.

C.J. Barnes stood up, swept the crowd with a smile, and announced his text. "Tonight we will consider Romans 14:12: 'So then everyone of us shall give account of himself to God.'"

A memory stirred in Lee William's mind. Ben's words came back to him: "You're askin' God to do a lot of explainin'. I always thought it was the other way around. . . . I get kinda worried that someday God will want me to do some explainin'." He shook off the thought and concentrated on the preacher's next words.

"As soldiers we know what it means to give account of ourselves. As prisoners we live with the hope that one day we'll be rescued and our captors will have to give account for all the misery we've endured. We hope . . . but we don't know for sure.

"But there is one thing we do know. The Bible says we shall *all* give account—the poor fellow dipping water too close to the dead line, the rebel guard who shoots a thirsty man. Union or Confederate, one day we'll each give an account.

"The heart of a murderer or a thief can beat beneath a blue coat as well as a grey. God didn't make war—men did. God didn't bring sin into our world—men did. Friends, don't add to your misery by demanding that God explain this mess. Instead, prepare yourself to meet your Maker. If you're a believing man, trust him to get you through each day, no matter what it brings . . . "

The preaching over, Barnes invited those who wanted to pray with him to stay behind. Lee William waited until all the others had gone.

"You were preaching to me tonight. I've been adding to my own misery," he confessed.

"Ahh," acknowledged Barnes. "The soldier from the creek. I don't think I ever got your name."

"Chidester—Private Lee William. Beer's army. I've been demanding explanations . . . for a long time now."

"You're not alone, Chidester," said Barnes, shaking his head. "When things get hard, we all spend too much time asking God to explain the suffering and not enough time asking him to help us get through it."

He touched Lee William's shoulder, then let his hand rest there. "I can't help you with explanations, but I believe you can find help . . . if you've a mind to."

There was no hesitation. "I've a mind to. Tell me what to do. I know all about how He died for me, and I know when I die I'll go to my home in heaven. But seems like God's far away from me now. Andersonville stockade is so godforsaken . . ." Lee William's voice faltered, and he hastily wiped his eyes with his ragged shirt sleeve again.

Barnes was nodding sympathetically. "If you indeed are a believer, God is never going to forsake you—not even here in Andersonville. Don't ever forget that. When you wake up tomorrow morning, pray, 'Thank you, God, for another day that I'm alive. Thank you, God, that no matter what man does to me, you will never forsake me. Thank you for being here in Andersonville.'" Barnes paused a moment. "He is, you know. He is right here in this filthy stockade with you, with me. He never forsakes his own. Hold on to that!"

Lee William's eyes were moist as he looked into Barnes' face. "I was wondering," he said, "could we pray right now instead of waiting 'til morning?"

And the two knelt together.

CHAPTER TEN

On the Homefront

———— ❧ ————

Dogwood Creek, 1864

September was more than half gone before a letter arrived in Dogwood Creek, telling the story of a man changed—changed despite the problems around him that were unchanging. The morning that MaryAnn Chidester picked up her son's letter at Carrick's Mill the Missouri hills were ablaze with goldenrod.

She had driven the wagon, hauling one lone sack of corn to be ground at the mill. At the last minute, she had asked Lucy to spare Little John for the day, more for his sake than for hers. The child seemed to be hankering to go along. He proved to be good company. He was delighted to pick all the ripe fruit from a papaw bush near the spring where they stopped for a drink, and he didn't complain even once about the roughness of the ruts that passed for a road.

Later, MaryAnn worried that she had unnecessarily exposed her grandson to danger, for she learned at the mill that Sterling Price's men were marching through the area. Old Jason Carrick met her as she alighted from the wagon and tied the reins to a post. He wasted no time giving her the news.

Hoisting the sack down, he eyed Little John as if measuring him from head to toe. "Anybody on your place big 'nough to take the mules and hide 'em in the woods for a spell?" he asked. Then, without waiting for any reply, he blurted the news of a battle at Pilot Knob.

"Ewing's men held him off—even killed more 'n a thousand rebs before he pulled out. Ewing left nary a gun for Price. But I hear tell Price is headin' thisaway, on his way to St. Louis. It's none too good for folks in these parts." Jason paused and lowered his voice, as if the rebel soldiers might be lurking behind the nearest trees. "Price is looking for mules, horses. Might be his foragers will come this way to 'void the militia down Sullivan way. Don't mean to frighten you, ma'am, but these be a mighty fine pair of mules, and I'd hate to see the rebs take 'em away. Might be hard to come by 'nother pair."

MaryAnn thanked him kindly and gave Little John permission to go with Jason to grind the corn. She drew her list from her pocket and went inside the store.

Immediately Jason's wife handed her Lee William's letter, saying, "I hope it brings good news!"

So did MaryAnn. She took it eagerly—this was only the second letter to arrive since Lee William had been sent to the rebel prison in Georgia. Seeing that it was addressed to Lucy, she put it in her apron pocket.

"What about your boys, Mrs. Carrick?" she inquired. "Any news?"

"Both healthy and safe—last I heard of 'em. Guess a body can't ask for more." Mrs. Carrick was a chatty woman. "Is it true that Jacob Broom's taken to wearin' one of Martha's dresses and her slatted bonnet in the field?" she asked eagerly. "That's a right smart way to fool the rebs. They sure

68

wouldn't likely leave a man standin' in these fields, if they come."

MaryAnn fingered the letter in her pocket. "Well, there ain't hardly a man left on Dogwood Creek for them rebs to find!" she reminded Mrs. Carrick.

Mrs. Carrick seemed suddenly to recall that Lee William Chidester was a prisoner. She closed her mouth and turned to her work.

"Still no flour, no sugar," she said, shaking her head. "We got salt now, though."

"Good. We been doin' without," said MaryAnn, thankful that at least they still had plenty of molasses and meal to substitute for sugar and flour.

As Old Man Carrick loaded her wagon and lifted Little John up beside her, he cautioned MaryAnn again to stay off the main road. He promised to send news through the neighbors if he heard anything. "Until you hear Price's men are gone, keep these mules off the road, stay close to home, and keep the latchstring pulled!"

MaryAnn hurried the mules along, talking all the while to distract Little John. She hoped he would not notice that she continually searched the surrounding landscape as they traveled.

But he saw it at once. "Whatcha lookin' fer, Gramma?"

She looked at her small grandson with a mixture of pride and apprehension. For as young as he was, the boy was mighty quick to sense when something was wrong in the grown-up world. She evaded his question by asking him another—one that he was familiar with.

"Why are you and Papa and Grandma MaryAnn alike?" she asked.

"I know!" He bounced on the wagon seat. "I'm the seventh child of the seventh son of the seventh child . . . What does it mean, Gramma?"

She smiled at him. "Never mind. I've got a letter from your papa in my pocket. As soon as we get home, you can tell your mama the good news."

But when they came to the cabin, Jacob Broom and his son were there and MaryAnn forgot about the letter. Jacob had heard the news and had come to see if MaryAnn wanted Jacob Junior to take the mules to the woods for a time.

"But he's only nine," she protested. "I couldn't ask him to do that."

"He's got to go anyway. I'm bound to keep my one hard-earned work animal. She's old and stiff, but she's all I had the means for. I don't aim for the rebs to take her like they took my team when we lived down New Madrid way," replied Broom.

The words were hardly out of his mouth when Jacob Junior and Little John rushed to his side, both talking at once. "Cain't Little John come with me, Pa?" begged the older boy.

Lucy gasped, but Jacob Broom said immediately that would not be necessary. Grateful and relieved, MaryAnn agreed that as long as Jacob Junior was going with the horse, he could take the mules along.

Little John was quiet for a few minutes. Finally he approached Lucy.

"But Mama, won't Junior have any person with him in the woods? Won't he have no company 'cept for Gramma's mules?"

To MaryAnn's amazement, Lucy gave her son permission to go along. Then she cupped his chin in her hand and demanded that he listen to her.

"Can you mind Junior? Can you keep perfectly quiet so as not to call any rebels up? Can you sleep outside 'thout a house and a proper bed?"

Little John nodded bravely until the last question, to which he responded, "Might I take along my quilt?"

The grown-ups and older sisters laughed then, and Lucy took him by the hand, saying she'd help him fix a bedroll.

Jacob Broom declared that it would be best for them to leave at first light the next morning. He offered to take the wagon to the barn and then unhitch the mules and take them home with him.

"The boy oughta come 'long with us now, too," he added.

Little John looked stricken at this suggestion. "Do I have to go with them right now?" he cried.

Lucy knelt beside her son. "You changed your mind, Little John?"

"No, Mama," he insisted. He searched his grandmother's face, but MaryAnn looked blank.

"I want to stay home and hear my papa's words!" he blurted out then.

MaryAnn's hands flew to her pocket. "Mercy!" she cried. "Oh, Lucy, I'm sorry!" She pulled out the letter and handed it to her daughter-in-law. "With all the worry about Price's men, I clean forgot."

It was Lucy who suggested that they could read the letter while Mr. Broom tended to the wagon. As soon as he was outside, she tore open the letter, looking at it hungrily and then at MaryAnn expectantly.

MaryAnn took it and read every word aloud.

July 29, 1864
Andersonville Prison
My dear wife,
    I cannot but think of you day and night. I pray every
day that you and Mama and the children are well. I am
comforted knowing that you are praying, as ever, that
this war will soon be over and we will be together again.
    Food is scarce—and hardly fit to eat. Recently I have
developed a cough that hangs on. But last night I made
my peace with the Almighty, and so today everything is
different even though nothing has changed . . .

MaryAnn read on. Lee William had told the whole story of
meeting C.J. Barnes and of his new peace with God. She read
slowly, for a lump had risen in her throat and it was difficult
to keep her voice even.

Lucy openly wept. "I'm that glad," she said when MaryAnn
had finished. "I'm glad he's found his peace of mind." She
smiled at the children huddled together by her chair and
then hugged Little John close.

No sooner had they fixed his grubsack and bedroll than
the Brooms came back.

"Say your prayers, Little John," reminded his mama.
"Pray for Papa!"

"Yes, Mama," he said, standing straight as a stick. Then
he marched out the door, not once looking back.

CHAPTER ELEVEN

Russell's News

——— ∽ ———

Jacob Broom came by the Chidester house to report on the boys the next morning. The girls spied him first, for they were under the walnut tree stomping off the green hulls from the fallen nuts. They quickly surrounded him—all but Arial, who went at once to fetch her mama.

MaryAnn, hearing the ruckus, came around the house from the garden. She greeted Jacob, motioning to the chairs on the porch. Lucy came through the door and drew a chair near, hushing the children as she did so. Lucy was plainly eager to hear information about her son.

The boys had camped near a spring that flowed out of a cave. It was in a secluded area above Jubal Tate's cabin, past the end of the road. Jacob reported that the boys had tethered the animals downstream of the spring and had also placed their tin pails of grub in a branch of the spring, where they would remain cool. Jacob had left them there, after securing their promise not to build any fires at all, since rebs were sure to spot smoke.

The cave would serve as a perfect shelter—it was just high enough for the boys to stand in. There had been no signs of animals, and Little John had cleverly brought in leaves to keep the dampness from their bedrolls.

The mother and grandmother looked at each other, both feeling some relief. Little John was bright and resourceful, though young, and they knew he could be trusted.

Four days later Logan Bennett rode in with the news that Sterling Price and his men had gone west after raiding the militia camp in the next county.

"They fought for four days," reported Logan. "Sixty men dead, and no tellin' how much property damage. Some say it's near half a million. But he's gone now, and I reckon it's a mite safer about these parts."

"Hooray!" shouted Arial. "Little John and the mules can come home! Let's go tell 'em!"

Logan looked at Arial and then at Lucy and MaryAnn, a question on his lips. When they explained about hiding the mules, Logan gave a low whistle. "That's a mighty brave boy you got there, Miss Lucy," he said.

Meanwhile, Arial had been begging her mama to let her go and fetch Little John. But Lucy was afraid that she might get lost and suggested that maybe they should all go instead. MaryAnn jumped in, adding that they could stop by the Brooms on the way to pass the news.

Logan took his leave and was nearly out the door when he turned and drew a letter from his pocket. "I plumb forgot. Jason Carrick brought this letter for you when he come to tell me about Price." She saw that it was from Russell. Wishing she had time to read it, but knowing that the girls were too wiggly to wait for her and that the small boys were probably longing to come home, she said, "It's from your uncle Russell. I'll read it when we get back. Now s'pose we go fetch your brother."

The words were hardly out of her mouth before the children raced away toward their cabin where the Broom family now lived. They stopped only once to examine the apples in the orchard and then raced through the hilltop field and across the little creek to the cabin door. Lucy and MaryAnn, walking slower, arrived just as Arial was telling the Brooms that Sterling Price was "clean gone out of the country" and it was time to fetch the boys home again.

Junior and Little John were more than ready to come home, and—now that it was over—recounted every detail as though it had been a great adventure.

"Little John did right well," said Junior. "He's brave enough to be a soldier!"

The child stood tall at these words, but later, after a favorite supper of cornbread and fried apples and a good bath, he confessed to Mama and to MaryAnn that he had been frightened each night by the spooky call of the hoot owls.

The children safely in bed and asleep, MaryAnn took a moment to thank the Almighty for the safe return of her grandson and to pray for the safe return of the child's father.

It was then that she remembered Russell's letter and eagerly sat down to read it.

Opening the seal of the letter, MaryAnn breathed a quick thank-you to the Almighty for the safety and nearness of this son. The letter was a thick one, and she settled back to enjoy it.

Dear Mama,

I hope this finds you well and safe.

Two urgent matters prompt me to write. Uncle George may have written you that a man claiming to be Sean Brean was with him for two months or more—

Here MaryAnn caught up the page to read the words again. She looked up at the painting of her great-grandmother Brean, which hung as the family's treasure above the fireplace. "Oh, George," she whispered to the brother who lived far away in Indiana, "you did it! Your dream, Papa's dream. You finally brought over another Brean!" The young woman in the painting seemed to smile down at MaryAnn from her position on an Irish jaunting cart. *Soon the picture of great-grandfather could be hangin' on George's wall,* she thought to herself, *when the last Brean comes from County Cork.*

She returned to the letter.

It seems that this Sean Brean decided that he was entitled to half of George's farm, since it was also his great-grandfather who had homesteaded it. I don't know all the details, but I do know that George gave him a lot of money, and Sean agreed that it was a fair price. The very next morning he stole George's saddle horse. George hasn't heard from him since.

I have my doubts whether this man was really our cousin from County Cork.

Though MaryAnn scanned down the letter for more information about George and the Irish Breans, Russell had written no more about it. Her heart sank, and she immediately worried how her only brother was surviving this disappointment. She went back to Russell's statement that perhaps the man had not been Sean Brean at all. She shook her head in disbelief. She glanced at the painting again, this time thinking that a Brean could never treat another Brean in such a manner.

The letter continued with news of Lee William.

Lee William wrote me on September 15 from Andersonville prison. I trust his letters are getting through to Dogwood Creek. In case they are delayed, I will just tell you that my brother has finally quit worrying over how the Almighty fits into all the schemes of man and is concentrating on how we all fit into the plans of the Almighty. I am glad for that.

I am sorry to hear Lee William is quite sick with swamp fever and maybe even consumption. He writes that there are daily rumors of a possible prisoner exchange. This is probably because the Union army is closing in. Anyway, Lee William thinks he is too sick to be considered for exchange, though he said it might be possible he will be moved on a hospital car with other sick prisoners. He has no idea where they might send him.

MaryAnn again stopped to pray. "Almighty God, we can't lose track of him. It's enough that he's there and that we're here alone, tryin' to get by without him. Please, God . . . "

Russell's next words took her by surprise.

I have decided to come home in time for early plowing in the spring. Mr. Eads has agreed that I can take leave

77

until the war is over. Most of the work is done for this season, so I'll be there after winter. Lee William has asked me to come.

A feeling of relief rushed over her and MaryAnn almost laughed out loud. Things had been good between her and Russell since his last visit. She remembered the pain of their argument, but more often she remembered the comfort that came with the resolving. Still, she would never have expected him to come to Dogwood Creek. Then again, she reasoned, Lee William had asked him to come.

She laid the letter aside, pondering once again how Russell and Lee William had looked out for one another since boyhood. If Lee William decided that Russell was needed on Dogwood Creek, then of course Russell would come.

CHAPTER TWELVE

A Long Winter

———— ❦ ————

It was a bad winter on Dogwood Creek—the worst since the year William John had died, although the fever didn't come. All the Chidesters were well—except for MaryAnn. She felt poorly much of the time and her frequent coughing nearly wore her out.

Snow had covered Dogwood Creek by November, when Mr. Lincoln was reelected, and it had barely thawed by the time he was inaugurated in March. In the months between, Mary-Ann never once made it to Carrick's Mill, for the wagon ruts had frozen over and travel was impossible. Logan Bennett occasionally made it through, bringing back the few available supplies, some mail, and newspapers for the Chidesters.

Every time Logan came by, Little John ran to the door, asking for a letter from his papa. When none came, he satisfied himself by saying, "Papa is too busy being a soldier." Afterward, he would play soldier himself, marching about the cabin with a piece of kindling in one hand, as if he were fighting with his papa in Mr. Lincoln's army.

Wishing her husband, the real teacher, were there to do it himself, MaryAnn got out his books and did her best to hold school for the children near the fireplace. She fought to control the coughing spasms that interrupted their lessons, and though she felt better on some days, the cough never went away.

MaryAnn read the papers eagerly, searching for every encouragement that the war would soon be over. Her hopes soared in January when the generals of both armies met together under a white flag to discuss the terms of a treaty. Then January faded into February. And though the talks failed, MaryAnn's hopes did not. The newspapers reported that the rebel armies were in retreat everywhere except before Richmond. Surely they could not hold out much longer.

———

One March morning in 1865, MaryAnn restlessly thrust aside the dress she was patching. "There's more patch than dress!" she complained to Lucy. "I declare, if it wasn't for this war and things bein' so scarce, I'd make a mop outta this one!"

They talked briefly of recent events and how it looked like the war was almost over. But neither spoke of the fact that not one letter had come from Lee William all winter.

Tired of the confinement of the cabin, Maryann put away her patching, drew on her cloak, and escaped to the woods. She made her way directly to the schoolhouse and stopped before the grave of her husband, where she had stood so bitterly a few years before. She stood, for fear that kneeling on the damp earth would only aggravate her cough.

"Things will be better soon, William John," she said quietly. "War's nearly over they say. We don't know where Lee William is, and it's been so long . . . but he'll be home by and by I expect. Russell's comin' home soon for plantin' time . . ."

As if her words could really make it happen, she turned at the sound of footsteps crunching in the snow. There she saw the lone figure of a man approaching.

"Russell!" she called. "I'm so glad you've come, Son!"

He ran the last few steps and hugged his mother close. "Lucy told me I'd find you here. She also tells me you've had a bad cough all winter. What are you doing out in this cold, Mama?"

"The sun is shinin' right nice today, Son. Look!"

"No matter, Mama. It isn't that warm yet. Come on, let's go back to the house. Lucy has some hot coffee for us."

As they walked through the woods, Russell asked about Lee William and was not surprised to learn that the family had received no word from his brother all winter. "Uncle George says he thinks Lee William's been sent to a prison hospital somewhere closer to the Mississippi."

"You've seen George?" MaryAnn queried.

"No. He wrote me in St. Louis. He's as worried as you are. He's been checking all the papers for notices on where prisoners are being held for transporting."

"What else did he say?" prodded his mother.

"That's all. To tell you the truth, most of his letter was about other business—about Sean Brean."

"What! Did the man come back?"

"No, and Uncle George never got his horse back, either. The fact is, I wrote to him first because of something I overheard on the docks one day. Uncle George says he aims to look into it."

He paused, and MaryAnn impatiently wished he would get on with the story. "So?" she asked.

"I was doing some business with the captain of a steamship—it was the *Sultana*—while it was docked in St. Louis, and I heard one boathand tell another that he had made an easy few hundred dollars by being in the right place at the right time. I didn't catch everything he said, but I did hear him say he'd gone to Indiana to claim half a cousin's farm. The other man said, 'I didn't know you had kin in Indiana," and then they both laughed.

"Uncle George had written me that after Sean Brean left Indiana, George inquired at the village and discovered that Sean had asked some questions about a store poster advertising jobs in the Cairo boatyards. The *Sultana* makes regular stops at all the ports on the Mississippi, so I thought George ought to check into it."

MaryAnn looked puzzled. "But what could George do? It'd be a mite hard to find a man that's travelin' up and down the river on a boat."

"Not any boat, Mama. All George has to do is check the steamship notices for the port schedule for the *Sultana*. I'm sure he could enlist the captain's help if he asked. I hope he does look into it. Uncle George is a bit too soft—that's why he got swindled in the first place."

Russell did not speak harshly. Still MaryAnn did not take kindly to any criticism of her brother. "You know he would have done anythin' to help Sean Brean and his brother," she said defensively. "He's bent on bringin' the family over from Ireland."

"The family, yes, not the rest of Ireland."

"What do you mean?" she asked.

"I think the man was an impostor. I'll wager he's no kin of ours." Russell sounded adamant.

MaryAnn thought for a moment before asking, "Did you get a look at the man on the steamship?"

"Yes. And he fits Uncle George's description right down to his red handlebar mustache. But the captain told me he goes by the name of Jake O'Reilly on the *Sultana*. Works as a part-time barkeeper and a boathand."

"Was his hair red, too?" MaryAnn asked.

"Mama, usually a man with a red mustache has red hair."

"Well, did he?" she persisted.

"Of course!"

MaryAnn nodded. "Russell, you're right! He can't be a Brean—all Breans have hair black as coal." She pushed her own back. "Well, at least 'til it turns grey."

"Seems to me you've had more than enough to turn your hair grey this winter, Mama," said Russell kindly.

"Never mind that. I'm surprised at your Uncle George. He should have known that man was an impostor the moment he set foot in the door. There's no Breans with red hair as far back as anyone can remember."

"So where's the real Sean Brean, then?" Russell wondered aloud.

"And why would this O'Reilly person go to Indiana, pretendin' to be him?" echoed his mother.

"George will want to find out. Most likely, he'll meet the *Sultana* at some port first chance he gets. He said in his last letter he was already looking for someone to tend the farm . . . which isn't easy with everybody fighting the war."

"Sounds like George is set on findin' this red-headed fellow who calls himself a Brean," MaryAnn responded.

"That's not all, Mama." Russell threw his arm around his mother as they walked. "He's set on finding out what he can about Lee William, too. He's planning to check every possible lead." He paused, searching MaryAnn's lined face, which looked old and frail in the bright sunlight. Then, as if hoping to encourage her, he said, "The newspapers say it can't be long now 'til Lee is defeated. Grant is closing in. It'll all be over soon, Mama. You'll see."

CHAPTER THIRTEEN

The Plan

❧

April 14, 1865

In his hotel dining room in Cairo, Illinois, George Brean sat reading a copy of the *Cairo War Eagle*. He scanned the news. There were continued reports of Lee's surrender five days ago at Appomattox. Suddenly he set down his coffee cup with a splash. There, on the front page, was the notice he was looking for!

The regular and unsurpassed passenger packet Sultana *in command of Captain J. Cass Mason departs tomorrow at 10 o'clock in the morning for New Orleans, Memphis, and all way landings. The* Sultana *is a good boat as well as a fleet one. Mr. Wm. Gamble has control of the office affairs while our friends Thomas McGinty and James O'Hara will be found in the saloon, where everything of the "spirit" order can be had in due time.*

George read carefully, memorizing each detail of the notice. *So, the Irish are givin' out spirits in the saloon,* George mused. *Well, if my information is correct, I bet there's another*

Irishman there to help 'em! It's been a long time comin', but I'm gettin' to the bottom of this O'Reilly business!

Since the *Sultana* was not departing until the next day, George lingered over his meal, reading the paper more carefully. He scrutinized the war information for ideas on where to locate his nephew. His glance was arrested by an advertisement offering the latest in sheet music, "Bring Me a Rose from His Grave." He crumpled the paper angrily and tossed it aside. Some Broadway composer was reaping a profit from the casualties of this detestable war, while his own nephew could very well be one of them.

But even as the paper fell to the floor, a casualty list caught his eye. He retrieved the page and smoothed it out. He searched the list carefully, hoping that he would not find his nephew's name among the known dead. When Lee William's name was not found on the list, George sighed heavily. "At least there's still hope. He's gotta get home to his family!"

At length, he laid the paper down, paid for his breakfast and left. He spent an hour walking unfamiliar streets before returning to his quarters to arrange for another night's lodging. Then he made his way to the riverfront, where he booked a passage on the *Sultana*. His plan was to get on board, confront Jake O'Reilly, and discover what happened to the real Sean Brean. If his plan worked, he would have his answer before the *Sultana* headed back upstream. Beyond that, he hoped to get off the ship at St. Genevieve and head west toward Dogwood Creek and his sister.

———

Shouts of newsboys hawking papers in the street awakened him early the next morning. He went to his window and threw it open to satisfy his curiosity about the early morning commotion. Even from the second-floor window, he could read the large words: "NATIONAL CALAMITY!"

"You down there!" he called to a sandy-haired boy. "What's happened?"

"Read it fer yerself, mister," replied the boy smartly. "Wanna buy a paper?"

"Of course, of course. Meet me at the door!" George pulled on his trousers hastily and hurried down the stairs. Now sure of his sale, the boy offered politely, "The President's been shot."

George paid the boy and collected the paper. Back in his room, he read the details. Secretary of War Stanton had sent a telegraphed message: "Abraham Lincoln died this morning at 22 minutes after 7 o'clock." Shaken by the news, George readied himself solemnly. Somewhere in the distance he heard church bells ringing and a cannon crashing.

He ate his breakfast quickly, paid his bill and hurried through town past storefronts that were already draped in black and posted with signs: "Closed for the day." The cannons boomed again.

George found everything in confusion at the waterfront. It seemed obvious that the day's excitement would delay the ship's planned departure time of ten o'clock. He sat on an overturned crate and kept an eye on the dock activities.

He had carried the *Cairo War Eagle* with him, hoping that now he'd have an opportunity to read it from front to back. A small item on page four turned all his plans upside down.

Several thousand Union prisoners of war released by the Confederate army are currently detained in an exchange camp near Vicksburg awaiting processing for final release from duty.

He searched the paper carefully, but found no further information. By midafternoon he found himself face to face with Captain J. Cass Mason on the *Sultana's* deck as the ship moved away from the landing.

"A great ship, sir," began George.

"Thank you. I've got a small share in her," confessed the congenial captain, after explaining some of the finer points of the ship. George moved restlessly. "You look like you've got something on your mind," the captain continued.

"Yes, sir—two things!" said George excitedly. "First, when do we get to Vicksburg? I want to get off there and catch you on your way back upriver."

"Of course. Should be there by Tuesday late. So far as the return, I expect to be there on schedule the following Sunday. Time enough to do your business?"

George nodded. "That'll do just fine. I read about the Union prisoners of war being held there for processing before release. I'm trying to find news on my nephew."

"This war's a dreadful thing." The captain was sympathetic. "Now, is there anything else that I can do for you?"

"Oh, yes. Do you have one Jake O'Reilly workin' on your ship? Maybe as a deckhand and part time in the saloon?"

The captain looked surprised. "Your information is quite correct. And I might add that Mr. O'Reilly has done a commendable job for us as a deck hand. The saloon, of course, is a private concession and they handle their own business affairs. Perhaps Mr. McGinty could help you. This O'Reilly—is he a friend of yours?"

George hesitated, not knowing how much information to give the captain. "The truth is, sir, he once posed as my cousin, recently come from Ireland. He beat me out of a great deal of money."

"And you want your money back. I can understand that! Perhaps Mr. Gamble, our office man, can assist you. He handles the pay."

"Of course I am interested in getting what money I can retrieve. But I am even more interested in knowing what happened to my real cousin . . . but it's a long story, and I can tell you have business to attend to. Thanks for your help, Captain."

"Well, if you need my assistance in the matter, feel free to contact me. I will say that he has been a good hand. Perhaps our O'Reilly is not the same man who cheated you."

"Perhaps not," said George politely. With a touch to his hat, the Captain strode away. George remained on the deck until sunset, enjoying the view as they chopped along the channel through Kentucky and past New Madrid, Missouri.

After a light supper, he wandered into the saloon, hoping for an opportunity to confront Jake O'Reilly. But the evening crowd was too thick. George gave up his search for the night and retired to his berth.

He slept anxiously in his bunk all night and woke early, before sunup. Once again he moved to the deck. They were due in Memphis before noon, and George knew the hands would be busy preparing to dock. He withdrew to the dining area, ordered a substantial breakfast, and bided his time.

Shortly before noon, as George was crossing the *Sultana*'s deck, he whirled about at the sound of a loud voice calling, "This way, O'Reilly!"

Two deckhands came rushing by, almost knocking him over in the process. "Beg pardon, sir! In a dreadful hurry here!" one of the men shouted over his shoulder.

The brief sighting was enough for George. He recognized the deckhand as the man who had come to Indiana, claiming to be Sean Brean.

George lost sight of Jake O'Reilly after the boathands rolled the gangplank into place. The crowd exploded, running off the ship and shouting the news of Mr. Lincoln's death. The people on the wharf mixed quickly with the crowd from the *Sultana,* and George decided it would be best to keep out of sight so that the impostor wouldn't recognize him until the time was right. He went to his quarters, determined to devise a plan.

The opportunity came midafternoon on Monday. After much thought, George sought out and explained his business with Jake O'Reilly to the ship's accountant, Mr. Gamble. Like the captain, Gamble said that O'Reilly had been an excellent hand on the *Sultana.* Still, Gamble admitted that he had in fact had some suspicions that O'Reilly might be hiding for some reason.

"I'm going to call him in. Wait here, sir," Mr. Gamble said. He immediately stepped to the door and called a cabin boy to fetch Mr. O'Reilly. Then, stepping back into the room, he invited George to have a seat.

George looked about the cramped quarters and took a chair near the door. Fifteen minutes later a heavy knock came, and Gamble called, "Come in."

"You wanted to see—" The words were barely out of his mouth when O'Reilly spotted George. He spun on his heel and made for the door.

With a quickness his nephew Russell would have been proud—and amazed—to see, George stepped between the crook and the door. Gamble rose to his feet.

"Sit down, Mr. O'Reilly," ordered Gamble. "This gentleman says you owe him a lot of money. Perhaps we can work out a payment schedule between the three of us."

O'Reilly's response wasn't what George expected. He didn't even protest. Instead, he stared at the floor, not saying a word. Then, turning to look George directly in the eyes, he laughed out loud. "I do owe ye some money. B'gory, it was easy money while it lasted. Ye were that easy to fool. Sure, and ye have me now dead to rights. Give me a coupla months and ye'll have yer money!"

"Good. Fine," said George quickly. "But I want to know what happened to the real Sean Brean. How did you know to—"

But O'Reilly was too fast for him this time. He bolted out the door and was gone.

"Never mind, Mr. Brean," said Gamble. "He can't go anywhere. And he seems reasonable enough. I don't think he's likely to leave this job. So just leave your address with me. I'll see that your money comes out of his pay."

"Thank you, sir," replied George uneasily. "But I've got to talk to that man, and I'll do it if I have to hogtie him to the deck!"

"As you wish," said Gamble, rising from his chair. Taking this as a signal that he was being politely dismissed, George rose and left the room.

O'Reilly's actions had convinced George that he knew something about the real Sean Brean. But O'Reilly was slippery. After the confrontation in Gamble's office, O'Reilly managed to avoid George. Somehow, he had to revise his plans if he were ever to get any information on his missing cousin. By the time they docked at Vicksburg, he had a plan.

It was Tuesday, just hours before their scheduled docking at Vicksburg, when George went once more to Gamble and Captain Mason. He warned the captain and Mr. Gamble not to let O'Reilly know he'd be boarding again when the *Sultana* came back through Vicksburg. He hoped to catch O'Reilly when the deckhand was confident that he had escaped the confrontation.

When the *Sultana* docked, George made quite a display of leaving the ship. He pushed his way through the departing passengers until he came to where he was in full view of all the deckhands. Then he noisily declared, "Let me off of here! I've had 'nough of this packet to last me a lifetime!" Rudely shoving his way, he left the *Sultana* and headed for the levee.

CHAPTER FOURTEEN

Progress at Last

George Brean swung his carpetbag over his shoulder and hurried ahead, darting beyond the other passengers. Then he deliberately slowed, choosing a path in full view of the *Sultana* to give O'Reilly every opportunity to see him leaving the ship.

Leaving the levee area, he climbed a winding brick road up into the city. There he booked a room at a hotel until Sunday, when the *Sultana* would return.

"Room 12, sir, just around that corner," the clerk said and held out a key.

George took the key but then hesitated.

"Could you direct me to the holdin' camp for Union prisoners?" he asked the clerk. "I'm hopin' to find my nephew."

"That'd be Camp Fisk," the clerk replied. "Go east on the four-mile road. The camp is right near the railroad trestle they call 'Four-mile Bridge.' Better hire a buggy—it's four miles from here. The livery stable's right down this street."

Ten minutes later, his carpetbag deposited in his room, George headed toward the livery stable.

As he boarded the buggy and took up the lines, he felt quite cheered by the prospect of the jaunt and the chance to see more of Vicksburg. But as he looked about, he found nothing cheerful in the surroundings. There were reminders of battle everywhere—earthworks, shell craters, bullet-scarred trees, boarded-up stores. Towering behind the city's church spires and chimneys, the great bluffs that had made Vicksburg such a Confederate stronghold were visible. Gaping caves dotted the bluffs. George remembered newspaper reports from the siege in the summer of 1863. The people had camped and hidden in those caves.

Below him, the serpentine Big Black River wound through a barren swath of land. Somewhere along that river, he knew, there would be a pontoon bridge that had been built by Grant's engineers. This bridge had allowed Union troops to enter the city by the back way. Driving the southern troops into the fortresslike city, the Union had starved them into surrender after a forty-seven day siege. The very thought of hiding in a cave for forty-seven days made George shiver.

As the buggy rolled along the road through the city, George passed several tight knots of people along the way. Almost everyone looked up as he went by, but none raised a hand in greeting.

So intent was he with his observations that he missed a fork in the road and found himself hopelessly lost. George started to speak to a group of old men who were so deep in conversation they had not yet noticed him, but he held his tongue when they abruptly stopped speaking and stared down the road.

George looked in the direction of their gaze. A lone Union soldier was approaching the group. The silence grew heavy. Some of the elderly men glared; others shifted their gaze to the sky. One noticed George and watched him as if waiting to see how he would identify himself.

George returned the stranger's intense gaze and, choosing his words carefully, spoke. "Lee's surrendered. It's time we all be friends."

No one answered. The soldier, who had taken it all in, approached George's buggy. "You a stranger here, mister? May I be of service?"

"I seem to have lost my way. I'm lookin' for the road to the prison exchange camp. There's a chance my nephew's among the prisoners. His last known location was Andersonville prison."

"I wish you luck, sir. I can show you the road, and I can tell you there are a lot of men down there from Andersonville. But you might have a hard time finding him even if he's there. There are almost two thousand troops in the exchange camp. Can't always keep the records straight."

One old man stepped away from the group and came near. He stood scratching his beard for a moment and then, shooting a contemptuous look at the Union soldier, asked George, "Do ye know fer sartin yer nephew's at the camp?"

"No. But I'm not passin' up the chance to look for him."

"Mebbe ye'd orter go to the hospital first. Taint out of yer way none. Mebbe ye'll find him there. Save yerself some trouble."

George looked questioningly at the soldier. He shrugged and admitted, "It's worth a try. I'll ride along, if you'll allow. Perhaps I can be of some help."

"Much obliged," said George as the soldier climbed up. George nodded his thanks to the old man, and they were off in the buggy again. Turning to the soldier, he said, "I'm George Brean."

The young soldier introduced himself as Captain Taylor, United States Army. "You'll have to forgive these people," Captain Taylor stated. "Here we're the enemy. The siege was hard for this town. Stores closed . . . food costs were impossible. Word was that flour went to two hundred dollars a barrel. 'Course it got to fifteen hundred in Richmond last month.

"See that monument, Mr. Brean?" Taylor continued, pointing to a granite shaft barely visible in the distance. "That's the site of the talk between Major General Grant and Lieutenant General Pemberton on July 4 of '63."

"Where the battle for Vicksburg officially ended?"

"The very spot. Soldiers from the national army put it up last year on the anniversary of the surrender of the city."

The two fell quiet for a few moments, and soon they came to the hospital.

"What's the name of your nephew?" Taylor asked as they went in together.

"Chidester. Private Lee William Chidester of Missouri. Last he wrote was from Andersonville prison. But it's been a long time, so we don't rightly know if—" George left the dreadful thought unspoken. He didn't want to talk about the possibility of Lee William not being alive.

The captain requested a list of patients from a nurse, who told them to wait. George looked about him. They were obviously understaffed to handle such an influx of patients. Doctors and nurses looked weary.

"First time in a troops hospital?" asked Taylor.

"Yes. I was just thinking that it's supposed to be over," George said quietly, "but the smell of death is still all around us."

"It's been bloody," responded Captain Taylor. "I for one will be glad to be home. It may be soon. They're planning to release all Union prisoners at the holding camp and send them home. Most will be sent by steamer up to Cairo, where they'll be mustered out. Perhaps you'll find your nephew among those being released."

"You expect the release to be soon?"

"Maybe within the week."

At the moment, the nurse reappeared, a sheaf of papers in hand. "What was the name you were looking for?"

"Chidester. Private Lee William." George tried to read the list she held.

She ran her finger down the columns. She had nearly exhausted the pages when she stopped. "Here we have it. Ward 'O'—I haven't tended those men much. Most came from Andersonville after they evacuated that filthy stockade. These were the ones who were too sick to march."

George interrupted her. "Can I just go and see? Can I go see if it's my nephew?"

"Forgive me," she said. "Of course."

They found themselves in a room filled with so many cots there was barely space to walk. Two nurses moved among the cots, handing out medicine and talking cheerfully to patients. The nurse led them to a far corner of the room, where she stopped beside a cot near a window. "Is this the man you're looking for?" she asked. A look of pity crossed her face.

An emaciated form lay on the cot. The nurse gently touched his shoulder. Hollow eyes opened, and the skeleton-like soldier looked up at George Brean and smiled.

CHAPTER FIFTEEN

Reunion

———— ❧ ————

George!?" cried the patient. "Is that really you?"

George fell to his knees beside the cot and wrapped the ghostly form in his arms. Lee William grasped his uncle and buried his head on the farmer's strong shoulder. The sound of the two men sobbing caught the attention of patients and nurses alike. Presently, George looked up to find every eye in the room fixed on them. For a moment, he returned their gaze, not knowing what to do. The bedridden soldiers smiled, but none spoke. George sensed that they were waiting for an explanation.

"It's my nephew . . . I've found him!" George shouted. He smiled back at the gaunt faces. Across the room a soldier cheered, and little by little the rest of the men joined in. Lee William lifted a bony arm and waved. As one, the group responded with a loud cheer.

When the cheering subsided, the nurse and Captain Taylor walked quietly away, leaving George alone with his nephew. He pulled a stool close to Lee William's cot and sat down.

"Oh, lad, it does me good to see you—even if I can barely recognize you! What can I do for you? Are you gettin' enough to eat?"

Lee William gave a soft laugh. "I reckon I could eat more if I had it. But on the other hand, it's a sight more than we had in the stockade."

"From the looks of you, I'd say the stockade was none too easy."

"But George," insisted Lee William, "I'm so much better." He coughed violently. "I'm afraid I've got slow consumption. What about you—what are you doing here in Vicksburg?"

"Lookin' for you, of course." George smiled.

"You come all the way to Vicksburg to look for me? Who's minding the farm?"

"Widow Reed's two boys."

Lee William whistled. "They were just tots when we left Indiana!"

"That was eleven years ago, Lee William. If the war had lasted another year, the oldest would've gone for a soldier." George hesitated a minute, studying his nephew's wan face. He decided to tell the whole story. "Actually, I came lookin' for someone else as well."

For the next half hour Lee William listened intently while George related his endeavors to confront the impostor-cousin Jake O'Reilly aboard the *Sultana.*

"I'll be gettin' back on that boat when she comes through on the upriver trip," he explained. "I aim to get to the bottom of this. I'm not quittin' 'til I know what happened to the real Sean Brean!"

Lee William smiled, comforted by the familiarity of his uncle's passion for the family dream. "Well, maybe I won't be

100

far behind. I guess we're all going home soon. And it can't be soon enough for me!"

"You'll have to go to Cairo first?" asked George, remembering what Captain Taylor had told him.

"I think so. We get our muster pay there." His face lit up. "I'm hoping there'll be enough to clear the farm."

"Lee William, I was hopin' you might consider comin' back to Indiana. I never wanted any of you to leave. It's been a hard life out there for the women, and your ma's not so young anymore."

"You've got one thing right, uncle—it's been a hard life. Seems as if life on Dogwood Creek is just one big hard row after another. But I reckon we're there to stay. It gets in your blood. Russell hates it . . . thinks it's too far from the railroad and thinks that Dogwood Creek won't ever change. But Ma and me—we don't mind. Don't have time to think about outside things when you're working a rock farm. We love working that land."

"And Lucy? How's she takin' to it?"

"Lucy? She feels right at home. She's been happier than she's been since she married me and settled down in Indiana . . . except when our other baby died. But having Little John made up for a lot of hard things." Lee William's eyes clouded at the thought of his only living son. "He'll be grown so when I see him again. . . . It's for him, Uncle George, that I want to own that farm free and clear. I want that farm for Little John . . . and so does Mama."

George nodded. "S'long as you 'member that you'd all be most welcome at the family farm—if ever the need be. I'm all alone. And after all this with Sean Brean—or Jake O'Reilly or whoever the man is—I'd rather have it that way 'less you Chidesters come back."

"I'm sorry about the money you lost, uncle."

"Money! That's not the half of it. 'Course it was money I could hardly spare, but the worst was thinkin' I was finally goin' to do what my own papa and his grandfather had tried to do. Turns out, I didn't do no better'n they did! My first thought when I found out I'd been duped was that I failed Papa." George Brean shook his head. "Maybe that's why it gets me so. I've been tryin' to make Papa's dream come true. I told your mama once that it's a heavy load to be responsible for somebody else's dream. I told her ever' person should have his own dream."

"I reckon you're right on that, George. Still, it's hard to separate," Lee William said. "Your papa's dream sort of became yours. My own dream is simple. I just want to get home again and be well enough long enough to get that farm in shape. In a way, maybe that's taking responsibility for Little John's dreams . . . and he might have dreams of his own." Lee William was silenced by a long spell of coughing.

"Enough for now," said George, realizing the visit had tired his nephew. "I'm goin' to scare up some extra provisions in town. Rest now, and I'll be back tomorrow."

———

A faint scent of magnolia blossoms hung in the air as George stepped into the quiet Sabbath evening. He breathed the pleasant odor deeply, then began to whistle softly as he walked briskly toward the hospital. Since finding Lee William, he had spent every day at the hospital. But this would be his last visit with his nephew, for the *Sultana* had berthed at the levee that afternoon, and he would be leaving to head north in the morning.

It made his leavetaking easier for George to know that Lee William would shortly be following him north and that they would soon meet in Dogwood Creek. Indeed, the prospect of that meeting had almost made him forget about his business with Jake O'Reilly.

George met Captain Taylor hurrying down the hospital steps.

"Good evenin', Captain!" he called.

"Ah, Mr. Brean. Good evening and good news! We're sending a couple thousand troops home as soon as transportation can be arranged to Cairo. Private Chidester will be among them. I must go now to see about the arrangements!"

George broke into a broad grin and called after the departing soldier, "Thank you, sir!" Then he bounded up the steps and down the hall toward Lee William's room.

George found Lee William standing, gazing out the window near his cot. He turned at the sound of his uncle's steps.

"Lee William, you're lookin' a sight better'n when I first saw you here!" George called.

"And I'm feeling a great deal stronger—at least strong enough to go home." He smiled. "And the army's making plans for our passage to Cairo—" His words dissolved into a coughing spasm.

"I heard. I'm right glad for you, and for Lucy and your mama." He paused, choosing his words carefully. "You reckon you're strong enough for the trip?"

"Swamp fever's gone. I'm so much stronger now. I reckon this cough will be with me awhile, though." He turned back toward the window for a moment, then he spoke quietly. "I was standing here remembering. Somehow, hearing that I was going home soon made me think about all the miseries of this war ... the fighting and the stockade. I feared I'd never breathe fresh air again. I never dream about the fighting, but every night the first month I was here I dreamed I was back in the stockade."

He faced his uncle. "Uncle George, I never want to see anything so vile again in my life. It was a living human pile of refuse, if there ever was one. I never got used to the stench of that place. I used to try to imagine I was on Dogwood Creek, smelling the fresh air and listening to the night creatures. But after a while, I couldn't even imagine it anymore. It's hard to believe I'll be there soon."

Supper rations interrupted Lee William's solemn mood. After the light meal, George suggested they walk outside. They progressed slowly, with the young man leaning on the older man's arm for support. George was unusually silent, and Lee William eventually asked him about his thoughts.

"I read somethin' in the newspaper," explained George, "that this has been a month of wonderful triumphs and terrible tragedies—first the surrender and then the assassination. I'm addin' to that the fact that I found you here alive and now you're goin' home. Sorta makes my problems with Jake O'Reilly seem not worth foolin' with."

"Uncle! You're not thinking of giving up the chase?"

George shook his head. "I can't! I think O'Reilly knows somethin' about the real Sean Brean. I can't shake the feelin' somethin' terrible happened to Sean ... I don't ever expect to find him alive. But I'd like to find his younger brother and—"

"I forgot. What is his name?" Lee William interrupted.

"Casey Brean. He wrote to me and said he hadn't had but one letter from Sean since he left Ireland and that was from New York. Said that Sean was sick with ship's fever. Casey was plannin' to come to America himself as soon as he heard from me. If he didn't find his brother in New York, he was plannin' to come to the farm in Indiana without him." A look of shame stole over George's face. "I was so mad when I got that letter—I'd just had my horse and my money stolen from the man I thought was his brother—I wrote him and told him I got no use for any more Breans from County Cork!"

"You didn't?!" cried Lee William.

"I did," said his uncle. "And I got a letter back. Casey wrote me one more letter, sayin' that he didn't believe his brother was a thief and that he wouldn't be botherin' me again. That letter came from New York City."

"Can't you write him again?"

"Already did. But I don't think he ever got the letter, for I explained exactly what happened. If Casey had gotten that letter, he would've answered it. I'm afraid he's left New York, and God only knows where he is. It'll be a miracle if we ever hear from him again." George hung his head. "I sidetracked my own dream with that letter! But I'm goin' to keep hopin'. Would be nice to have him come to the farm."

Watching his uncle's face, Lee William determined to pray for that miracle for his uncle.

CHAPTER SIXTEEN

Overload

———— ❧ ————

The hour was growing late when George and Lee William turned and made their way slowly back to the hospital.

Once again they encountered Captain Taylor on the way.

"Mr. Brean, I'm glad you're still here," he said in greeting.

"Any news?" asked George.

"Yes, I'm glad to say. Private Chidester, your orders are to board the *Sultana* tomorrow!"

"The *Sultana,* sir?" asked Lee William. All three men smiled broadly.

"Thank you, Captain," said George. "It was kind of you to arrange for my nephew to be on the same packet I'm taking."

"Well, it's nothing personal," explained the captain, "although I'm glad for your sake. All the troops are going on the *Sultana.*"

"All the troops?" asked George, a look of dismay on his face.

"That's the plan."

"But that's two thousand men!" George protested.

"Well, that's an estimate. It's hard to be exact—confounded bookkeeping, you know. We'll get an exact count as they

107

board tomorrow." The captain hurried away then to consult with hospital officials.

A frown puckered George's brow. He glanced toward Lee William who still wore a smile and seemed lost in dreams of home.

"I'll be right back!" called George, dashing after the captain.

"Can I have a word with you, sir?" he panted, catching up with the officer.

"Walk with me."

Out of earshot of Lee William, George demanded somewhat angrily, "What do you mean you are sendin' two thousand men home on that steamer? Captain Mason himself told me they were licensed to carry less than 400—countin' the crewmen."

"I'm afraid that's not my concern, Mr. Brean."

"Surely there are other packets docked that could share the load?" George queried.

"Certainly, but it's a matter of business." The captain explained that the shrewd business manager of the *Sultana* had managed to contract for all the troops before the other steamers had a chance—the army would pay five dollars for each enlisted man and ten for each officer transported.

"I can't believe Captain Mason would allow it—" began George heatedly.

"Captain Mason doesn't have anything to say about it. The troops are going on the *Sultana* at the command of the United States Army. Even the captain of the ship can't countermand that. And now, you must excuse me."

108

Captain Taylor strode down the hall, leaving George alone, his eager anticipation of the next day's journey turned to apprehension.

———

Before George left Lee William for the night, the two came up with a plan to meet on board the crowded *Sultana* the next day. George would board early and then wait for Lee William at the top of the gangplank. George masked his anxiety and anger, not wanting to betray his concern over the crowded packet to Lee William.

As soon as he left the hospital, George marched directly to the levee, his anger mounting with each stride. He crossed the gangplank onto the *Sultana* and immediately spotted the clerk.

"Mr. Gamble!" he called. "Do you know what time we leave tomorrow?"

"Depends on the boilers."

"The boilers?"

"Yes, sir. She began having problems down south of Vicksburg, and captain's orders is not to leave until the boiler is repaired."

The news did nothing to ease George's anxiety. He made his way directly to the captain's office.

"Enter," the captain called in response to the knock. George entered the room and closed the door behind him. As the captain looked up from his desk, George noted the man's changed appearance—there were deep lines in his face.

"Mr. Brean." The captain remembered. "I see you've made it back. I trust your business in Vicksburg went well?"

"Sir?"

"Your business—looking for a son or someone?"

"Yes . . . a nephew, sir. I found him."

"About your other business, Mr. Brean . . . I'm afraid I have distressing news. I know I agreed to call in Mr. O'Reilly so that you could have a word with him in my office, but something has come up that I'm afraid will occupy all my time—"

"Yes, sir, I know. The troops. I heard at the hospital. My nephew is one of those who'll be on board."

"Well, then . . ."

"Beggin' your pardon, Captain," began George, not quite sure how to start, "but it's just that I keep rememberin' how you explained all the fine points of your ship to me. You said she's licensed to carry less'n four hundred. Aren't you placin' your passengers at risk?"

The captain jerked himself up ramrod straight, stuck out his chin, and answered, "I would not risk my passengers or my ship . . . it is not my doing. I have warned the officials of the danger. I have told them I can neither legally nor safely carry that many, but I am powerless against the army." He sank back in his chair again, as if wearied by the problem, then continued, "Mr. Brean, you can see that I have many things to attend to."

"Thank you, Captain," said George, shaking the offered hand. "I shall pray Godspeed for the journey."

"Yes, Mr. Brean. May God have mercy on us all."

The captain stopped George just as he was about to close the door behind him.

"Mr. Brean! I don't like to ask you, but would it be possible for you to give up your stateroom for the trip? There are more women and officers traveling than we have staterooms. It would mean sharing open deck space with the soldiers . . . " Captain Mason twirled the ends of his mustache.

"Please, Captain, give no more thought to it. I'll be anxious to stay with my nephew anyway. The voyage will not be easy for him."

Captain Mason touched the brim of his cap, and George accepted the unspoken thanks.

———

The next morning George waited at the top of the *Sultana*'s gangplank, searching among the hospital patients who headed the line of boarding troops. He quickly spotted Lee William, who was smiling and waving his arms. George waved back, but his joy was dimmed by the sight of the unbroken line of troops stretching down the levee. He forced a smile, determined to keep his fears to himself.

They settled together in a spot on the deck to watch the proceedings. George related to Lee William Captain Mason's regret that he could not help with O'Reilly. But he said nothing of their discussion concerning the overloading of troops. Nor did he mention the boiler problem, though he could hear the pounding and clanking of work in the boiler room from where they sat.

During the dinner hour, the clanking ceased. But the loading of the steamer did not—it went on through the evening and into the night. Lee William stretched out and slept, but George stayed awake, watching until the ship's deck filled. When it seemed there was no room left, still the men came—haunted faces peering from skin-covered skeletons, some hardly able to walk. Yet everywhere around him,

111

George heard men laughing and shouting to one another as they shuffled along to their appointed places.

They're happy, he realized, listening to the men call to one another, laughing. *So happy to get home to family they don't even know the danger.*

It was well past midnight before the *Sultana* left port. From stem to stern, from rail to rail, from top to bottom, the steamer was covered with bodies.

Needing to move his cramped muscles, George picked his way among the soldiers. At the rail he stumbled into the ship's clerk.

"Say there, Mr. Gamble. What's the passenger count?"

"Mr. Brean, when we reach Cairo this'll be the greatest trip ever made on Western waters," he said, coming close and speaking softly so as not to disturb the sleeping soldiers. "We have twenty-four hundred soldiers, one hundred passengers such as yourself, and our crew of eighty—not to mention the horses and pigs in the cargo area!"

"Perhaps you should say 'if we reach Cairo,' considerin' the *Sultana*'s licensed to carry less'n four hundred people."

"I'm sure there will be no problem. The boilers are repaired, of course."

"I wouldn't be so sure if I was in your place, Gamble. When you consider the number of folks on this ship, you'll have to forgive my skepticism 'bout the boilers."

Gamble offered no defense. He rubbed his forehead, stared for a moment out over the water, and then walked away.

George looked out over the sea of human bodies. "God have mercy," he whispered. "May God have mercy on us all."

CHAPTER SEVENTEEN

Disaster

⟋⟍⟋

Lulled by the rhythmic sound of the paddlewheels, George and Lee William slept. Early the next morning, Lee William explored the ship with a fellow soldier. George walked along the rail for a while, marveling at the difference a week had made in the appearance of the river. Spring rains had swollen the river far beyond its boundaries. Though the steamer had been churning upstream close to the shoreline, it was now angling off in a gradual course toward the opposite shore. Midriver, uprooted trees turned end over end in the rushing torrent.

The overloaded *Sultana* wobbled along, and George felt increasingly anxious about the voyage.

Lee William returned, and George waited with him as they watched a quartermaster making his way around the deck handing out the day's rations. Finally, he approached them with hardtack, coffee, and saltpork.

"I'm a civilian," George told him. "I'll go below and get breakfast." The quartermaster nodded and hurried on to the next group of hungry men.

"Give that saltpork and coffee to me, Lee William," George said. "There's no place to cook it here. Let me see what I can do."

In the saloon he sat at the long dining table and sipped steaming hot coffee along with crisp bacon and sweet rolls. Then, fingering a coin, he bargained with the chief steward. "My nephew is one of the soldiers bein' transported. He's not strong. The army gave them rations, but there's no way to cook 'em. Reckon I could trade you this ration of coffee and saltpork for some fried bacon and a cup of boiled coffee? I'll make sure the cup gets back to you."

The steward hesitated only a moment. "Put your money away. Just leave the rations . . . it's a fair trade."

"Thank you," George said.

Carefully balancing the coffee and bacon, George made his way toward the stairs to the boiler deck, where he nearly collided with an officer.

"Excuse me!" declared the soldier. "You haven't spilled your coffee, have you?"

"No, fortunately. It's for my nephew."

"And these are for my men," said the officer, noticing George's glance at his armful of rolls. "Perhaps I should go ahead of you. I have no coffee to carry. I'll clear the way. Another collision and your nephew may have to do without his coffee!"

Lee William took the provisions gratefully. George sat quietly, watching the other soldiers as his nephew ate his bacon and gulped down the cooling coffee. He expressed his surprise to Lee William at the way the soldiers around them laughed and enjoyed themselves, never complaining about the impossible rations or the crowded conditions.

"What's a little crowding, or a few days eating hardtack? The important thing is, we're all going home," explained Lee William. A few moments later he continued, not noticing George's somber mood, "Have you come up with a plan to confront Jake O'Reilly, Uncle George?"

"I'm hopin' to find him in the saloon—he works there sometimes. Maybe tonight I'll go in and talk to him."

But O'Reilly was nowhere to be found that day.

The next morning Lee William and his uncle woke early, just as the *Sultana* laid anchor.

"Where are we?" mumbled Lee William.

"Helena, Arkansas," replied George. "It sure looks different—more muddy than the downriver trip. What's all that ruckus at the rail?"

Groups of soldiers had gathered at the rail. Beyond, on the wharf, a photographer was setting up his camera. "I want a picture of the troops!" he called.

The men cheered.

"Two thousand troops from all over the country—all on one boat. I guess this is a historic occasion," laughed Lee William. But his words were nearly lost in a sudden surge of men rushing toward the rail.

George gasped. "They're goin' to capsize the boat!" Even as he spoke, the steamer lurched off balance.

"Move away from the rail!" shouted the captain. With the help of the officers on board, order was restored and the packet soon righted itself once more.

But George was uneasy all day. Midafternoon, while Lee William napped, he walked the ship's decks, scanning every spot where the deckhands might be, but there was no sign of the red-haired O'Reilly. He had only two days left to confront him. Discouraged, he returned to Lee William and sat down.

The sky grew dark.

"Looks like we're going to get wet, Uncle," said Lee William, raising himself up on one elbow.

God have mercy, thought George, mindful of the younger man's slowly regaining health.

Though the rainclouds threatened for several hours, the soldiers were spared the drenching. The sun came out, tinting the overhead clouds with evening color. The deck grew noticeably quiet. As dusk settled in, Lee William sat up, cleared his throat, and began to sing "Sweet Hour of Prayer." Others immediately joined him, and the impromptu vespers service lasted until the lights of Memphis appeared.

As the packet swung into port, the officers ordered all the men to remain on board. But even as they spoke, at least a dozen men jumped from the ship. They were running to the city by the time the gangplank was in place.

Three hours later, the ship's bell clanged a departure warning. It was after midnight when the ship left Memphis and began to move to the Arkansas side of the river, where it tied up at a coalyard. Lee William was sleeping in their small space on the deck—larger now since the soldier who normally occupied the next space was gone. George, fully awake, stood by the rail and watched as the roustabouts hoisted great burlap bags of coal to their shoulders and carried them aboard for the trip to Cairo.

The last of the coal was loaded, the planks were pulled up, and the boat swung sharply from the Arkansas bank. At midstream, the pilot straightened her up and began a slow center passage through the islands.

George gazed into the black, swollen river, noting that they were now at least five miles from either shore. Startled by a noise on deck, George looked up and caught his breath—three men were moving straight toward him. One of them was Jake O'Reilly!

George waited, hardly breathing. He leaned against the rail, hiding his face until the men drew near.

When they came alongside, he turned quickly and grasped O'Reilly's shoulder. "A word with you, Mr. O'Reilly!"

O'Reilly hesitated, making no objection at first. Then, in the semi-darkness, he looked into George's face and bolted. This time George was not to be taken by surprise. He jumped after him, grabbed him firmly by the arm and said, "I will be heard—"

But his words were cut off as an explosion ripped the air, and the ship burst into flames.

The force of the explosion carried George into the air. Just as he fell into the convulsing river, he saw a blur of crashing smokestacks and collapsing stairs. The deck split in two.

"Lee William! Lee William!" George screamed as the cold, dark water of the Mississippi rose to meet him.

Moments later in the water, he realized that he was surrounded by dead bodies and drowning men fighting over the bits of wood blown from the ship. At once, he was conscious of screaming women, children, and horses. But he was unharmed.

"Make way!" came a call from the ship's hull above him. A group of passengers was preparing to jump.

"Move aside!" he gasped to those swimming near him. "Clear the water near the ship to make room!" He grabbed a floating piece of the deck and paddled away from the area.

For over an hour George paddled about, searching each group of survivors to see if Lee William was among them. His hopes rose when a downriver steamer approached and laid anchor. He was one of the first to be rescued on the *Bostonia*, headed toward Memphis.

As the crew and passengers of the *Bostonia* pulled dazed survivors from the water, George watched anxiously. Soon the deck was crowded with those rescued, but Lee William was not to be found. All too soon the ship's bell clanged to signal the end of the rescue operations and the boat prepared to move full steam ahead.

"Please!" cried George, catching a deckhand by the arm. "We mustn't leave yet. My nephew . . . he has a wife and children . . . he can't have come through war and prison to be left to die in this river!"

The deckhand shook himself free of George's grasp and caught George's arms in a tight grip. "Take it aisy, mon!" he muttered.

George stood silent for a moment, comprehending for the first time how irrational he must appear. He relaxed under the deckhand's restraining grip. "Sorry, mister."

The deckhand had no time to respond, for another crew member called out, "Give a hand, mate!" George turned to see one final passenger being dragged aboard. He hurried to the spot and reached out to help.

"This poor devil's in bad shape," said the deckhand. "Let's find a comfortable spot for him." The deckhand looked to George to help him. George leaned close to look at the scalded face and gasped out loud.

"Your nephew?" asked the deckhand.

George evaded the question. "I'll see to him," he said. "Put him here in this corner."

The deckhand hardly had time to lay his burden down before he had to dash off to other duties, and George found himself alone, staring into the burned face of Jake O'Reilly.

O'Reilly was barely conscious. He moaned, and his lips began to move. George leaned closer to catch the whispered words. "May the Lord keep life in me until the priest comes," he repeated over and over.

George bent over O'Reilly's face. "Talk, O'Reilly. Talk!"

O'Reilly turned unseeing eyes toward the voice. "Are you a priest?"

"No. I'm the man you cheated out of five hundred dollars. Now tell me, what did you do to the real Sean Brean?"

O'Reilly looked as if he would sink into unconsciousness.

"Talk, man, talk," urged George.

And, for a few brief moments, Jake O'Reilly talked. As George had feared, the real Sean Brean was dead.

And by the time they reached Memphis, so was Mr. Jake O'Reilly.

CHAPTER EIGHTEEN

George's Search

⟨≈⟩

After three weeks, George gave up his search for Lee William. He took the first boat to St. Louis, and from there he rode the mail stage to Carrick's Mill on Dogwood Creek. There he got directions to the Chidester farm.

"Yes, yes," acknowledged old Carrick. "MaryAnn's been lookin' for you ever since your letter come a week ago. Go south on the main road for three miles 'til you come to a foot path what crosses the creek. 'Nother quarter mile there's a fork in the road. Take the right-hand way, and the next cabin's where you'll find your sister."

Before George walked a mile, he could see why his sister loved Dogwood Creek and was so determined to stay there. Wounded by grief and disappointment, George found a peculiar comfort in the wild beauty around him. He also recognized the signs of war. Old men and young boys worked the creek-bottom fields. Other fields were overgrown. Some houses seemed to be deserted.

"Thank God it's over, anyway," he said to himself. He pondered over Lee William's fate. "Don't seem right he could survive everythin' the Confederates did to him and then die because the Union army ordered too many troops onto one steamer."

Quickening his pace as he passed the fork in the road, he realized that it had been eleven long years since he had seen his only sister. Almost immediately a cabin came into view. George started toward the door, but then he caught a glimpse of a garden beyond the house and changed his direction. He knew his sister well enough to know where she would be on such a day as this one.

A moment later, he saw her. Intent on her work, she did not hear him coming, and neither did the small boy kneeling in the soft dirt beside her.

"Lee William's seventh child," George whispered to himself. He spoke aloud.

"Mornin', ma'am. I come to see if you needed a good hand, but it 'pears you already got one!"

The boy spoke first. He drew himself up and offered his hand. "I'm William John Chidester, the second, but you can call me Little John. What's your name?"

MaryAnn smiled at her grandson. "This is my brother, George Brean, Little John." Then, her eyes on George, she said, "So you've come . . . it's really you." She moved quickly toward him.

He grabbed her in a tight embrace as he asked, "How are you?"

"Better, much better—now that you're here, George." She coughed violently, though, and George frowned, remembering Lee William's consumptive cough.

"It's been a long winter," she hurried to explain, noticing his concern.

"You've had a few of those since movin' to Dogwood Creek. I'm sorry 'bout William John."

MaryAnn's eyes moistened at the mention of her husband's name. "He was a good man. And I reckon we had more years'n most folks, but I still miss him."

George shifted uneasily, remembering that he had bad news for both MaryAnn and Lucy. "Is Lucy here, MaryAnn?" he asked.

MaryAnn nodded and asked, "Do you have news?" When he didn't answer, she said, "Let's go in. I 'spect Lucy's busy with the housework."

George paused on the back porch to drink from the dipper in the water bucket. "Good spring water!"

"Yes," said his sister. "And Little John here is our water-boy."

George looked at Lee William's son and then back at MaryAnn. How could he speak frankly in front of the boy?

MaryAnn walked ahead of him into the house. They found Lucy in the kitchen. "I'm pleased to see you, Mr. Brean," she said shyly. "Kin I git you somethin' to eat?"

"Not now," George answered. Then, glancing nervously at Little John, he continued, "Why don't we all sit down? I'm afraid I've got bad news."

"Little John," Lucy said quickly, "reckon you can go outside and play for a spell."

"Yes'm," replied the boy and started for the door.

"Stay in the yard," she called as he slammed the back door.

The three sat around the table, and Lucy began to roll a small knot in the corner of her apron.

"MaryAnn, Lucy," George began, "I have recently come from Memphis. Three weeks ago, I was on the *Sultana.*" He looked at the women, noting that neither seemed alarmed by his announcement. "The steamship *Sultana*," he emphasized.

"Russell told me about the *Sultana,*" MaryAnn acknowledged. "Was you lookin' for the red-haired man that claimed to be Sean Brean?"

George stared at his sister, unbelievingly. "MaryAnn, have you had no news on the *Sultana?* Don't you ever get any newspapers here?" he demanded.

" 'Course we get newspapers," MaryAnn replied patiently. "We get a paper from St. Louis ever' week."

George drew a deep breath and began again. "And this paper from St. Louis, has it had nothing in it 'bout the *Sultana?*"

"Unless the *Sultana* has somethin' to do with Mr. Lincoln, the papers wouldn't report it I 'spect."

"Twelve hundred bodies floating all over the Mississippi and the papers don't report anythin' but the dead Mr. Lincoln!"

"What bodies, George? Please, just get on with it," Mary-Ann pleaded.

He told them then the story of his search for O'Reilly and the tale of the unfortunate *Sultana.* Lucy guessed the rest.

"Lee William was on that riverboat, wasn't he?" asked Lucy flatly.

"I'm afraid so," he answered softly, barely able to speak. He couldn't look at her. He gazed down at his hands and rubbed them together. The room was quiet for a few moments before he finished his account of his search for Lee William. He recounted Lee William's story of the long days of war and prison and illness. "And in the end it wasn't even the enemy that killed him—his own army managed to do that. It's criminal what they did!" He gripped the table's edge. "I'm sorry, Lucy, MaryAnn, I'm so sorry."

124

"But Mr. Brean, what makes you so sure he's not alive iffen no one's found his body?" It was Lucy who raised the question. George looked at her, surprised by this reaction. He saw a determined look in her eyes. She set her jaw and raised herself up straight.

"I don't know for sure, Lucy. But when that boiler blew, the ship was an instant inferno. By last count in Cairo, more than fourteen hundred passengers was thought to be dead. Only half have been accounted for. I 'spect every day they'll be accountin' for more."

"I'm obliged to you fer lookin' fer him," Lucy said bluntly. "I reckon now it's time to git dinner. Russell's here. He's in the far field and won't be in 'til supper time. Likely he'll be proud to see you." Then she swallowed and spoke slowly, emphasizing each word. "Mebbe I'll walk to my cabin this afternoon and see the Brooms. Likely they can find another house now. Likely I'll be needin' to get settled in afore Lee William comes home."

George stared at her and shook his head at his sister. After dinner, Lucy took her son by the hand and said to him, "I reckon I got some business with Mr. Broom, Son. Come along and you kin play with Bertie for a spell."

While Lucy's girls cleaned up the kitchen, George and MaryAnn sat in the parlor, talking quietly about the years since they had last seen one another. But their enjoyment of each other was dimmed by a shadow of loss. George told his sister the story he had pieced together from O'Reilly's last words.

"Sean was sick when his ship docked in New York. O'Reilly had a habit of meetin' Irish folk at the docks and talkin' 'em into taking rooms at his boarding house. He knew from the start that Sean was a dyin' man. He decided to stay with him and take whatever Sean had on him. Sean talked a lot 'bout the family in Indiana, and O'Reilly got the idea that he could pose as the cousin from County Cork."

"But he must have known he'd be found out," MaryAnn interjected. "How could he expect to fool you forever?"

"Don't think he intended to. But he counted on bein' able to fool me long enough to get some easy money."

"I'm sorry about that, George . . . and about your horse. I know how a man hates to lose a good saddle horse."

George smiled. "I reckon you do know about that!" He stared out the window. "The worst is that after O'Reilly left Indiana I got a letter from Casey Brean. I was so mad I wrote him back and told him I was done with the Breans from County Cork." He explained how he'd tried to write again. "But I reckon he's moved on by now."

MaryAnn nodded. "So now you don't know where he is. Is that what troubles you?"

"Unless he contacts me again, we've lost all contact with the one remainin' Brean from County Cork."

MaryAnn looked up at the painting of their great-grandmother Brean. "I don't reckon dreams always come true, George. Sometimes they're just not meant to be." Sadness had crept into her voice. She rose from her chair and stood at the window, where she saw her daughter-in-law and her grandson coming into the yard. "On the other hand, sometimes it's hard to let them go."

CHAPTER NINETEEN

Casey Brean

❦

In a dim corner of a river shanty somewhere on the Mississippi, a young man watched as a thin soldier tossed fitfully on the rude cot where he had lain for close to four weeks.

Unaware that he was being observed, unaware of his surroundings, the soldier groaned in half-consciousness. He inched his emaciated frame into a new position. Though the movement was small, it induced more pain. He groaned again. Suddenly he bolted upright into a sitting position and cried, "George!" Then, gasping with pain, he fell back onto the cot.

Private Lee William Chidester slept fitfully, for there was no escaping the dream. Clouds of black smoke rolled around him until he feared he would suffocate. The fire roared closer, and he stood paralyzed, not knowing where to go. In the light of the flames, he could see George. But just as he reached out for him, the form changed, and a woman with a baby stood in his place. The captain was helping her into a life-jacket, telling her, "You must jump! Jump!" Then everything faded except the captain's face peering from a great ball of fire and smoke. The fierce light and moving shadows distorted the face as it came closer and closer, screaming, "You must jump, soldier! Jump!" Lee William was powerless to obey the command. "George!" he screamed again.

A hand touched his shoulder, and from somewhere a voice said, "Take it aisy. Sure'n it's only a dream."

Struggling to open his eyes, Lee William murmured, "George?" And then, with a troubled frown marking his brow, he slept.

When the young man saw that the soldier was resting well, he rose and made a note on a scrap of paper: *May 23, 1865. The soldier shows signs of regaining consciousness.*

————

The next day Lee William awakened. He opened his eyes tentatively, wondering where he would find himself. He made no attempt to turn his head, but stared straight ahead. He was astonished at what he saw. There on the wall above his feet hung the painting he had seen so often in Mama's house. Satisfied that he was home in Mama's cabin, he closed his eyes, holding the vision of the jaunting cart and the Lakes of Killarney in his mind. He was almost asleep again when it struck him that something was wrong with the picture. He forced his eyes open again to examine the picture. Straining to concentrate, he saw that it wasn't Mama's painting after all. *Something's not right* . . . He slept again, puzzling over the painting.

————

He awakened again to the smell of boiling coffee. This time he turned his head to discover a tall young man with raven-black hair and a beard. Lee William stared at him, remembering the painting, and then gazed again at the wall at the foot of his cot. At last he saw what he had been searching for. In the painting, where there should have been a young woman in the jaunting cart, there was the figure of a young man. Even from where he lay, he could see the resemblance between the man in the painting and the young man beside him.

Lee William spoke his first slow words. "Who are you, and whose painting is that?"

"It's mine," the stranger replied with a great grin. "I'm Casey Brean . . . and that picture's of me great-great-grandfather."

Lee William jerked himself into a sitting position. For a moment, his head spun. *Casey Brean! Sean Brean?* The details of his uncle's story would not form themselves in his fuzzy thinking. He spoke again.

"I'm Lee William Chidester. My mama is the daughter of Ian Brean's grandson, Michael Leland Brean. For as long as I can remember, Mama has had a painting like that hanging in her home. But in her painting—"

"In her painting Great-great-grandmother Brean is in the cart." Casey finished his sentence.

Lee William nodded. Something triggered part of his memory and touched him with anger. "So you and your brother figured you'd cheat my uncle out of his farm in Indiana!"

"B'gory I didna do sech a thing!" Casey looked as though he had been struck.

"Half of it then."

"Sure'n I niver seen your Uncle George."

"Well, your brother Sean saw him. He came to the farm demanding that George pay him off or he'd claim half the farm."

129

Casey stared at Lee William with a bewildered look.

Lee William went on. "Sean figured that since Great-great-grandfather Brean homesteaded that farm, then half of it rightfully belonged to you and him. George finally agreed to buy him out."

"And yir uncle—he gave him money?"

"A *lot* of money."

"And where did Sean go then?"

"Disappeared the next morning with one of George's best horses."

"Sure'n that's not Sean. He wouldna be doin' sech things."

"How can you be sure?"

"Me brither's no thief."

Lee William felt suddenly tired and lay back against the pillows. Then he remembered more. "What does your brother look like?" he asked.

"Like me!" laughed Casey. "Only a stone or so heavier."

Lee William considered this, trying to remember what his uncle had told him. Casey Brean brought him a bowl of soup.

"Eat. Ye must git yir strength back," he urged, propping up Lee William with a rolled-up blanket behind his shoulders.

Lee William drank the broth eagerly and handed the bowl back to Casey. Then Casey brought two tin cups of coffee and handed one to Lee William.

"I'm obliged to you," said Lee William. Suddenly he remembered the whole story of Jake O'Reilly and his red hair.

"Does your brother have black hair, too?"

"Didna I tell ye he looks like me?"

"His hair's not red?"

"Red!" Casey roared with a rich laughter. "Sure'n, no Brean has red hair. As far back as we kin remember, it's black as coal, it is."

"Then that sure wasn't Sean Brean we saw on the *Sultana.*"

"What?" gasped Casey. "On the *Sultana,* ye say? On that burnin' inferno? 'Tis twelve hundred bodies it threw into the river, and one of them me own brither, ye say?"

"No, no!" declared Lee William. "Not your brother."

For the next half hour, Lee William related the details of George Brean's search on the *Sultana* for Jake O'Reilly, the man who had come to Indiana posing as Sean Brean.

"I'm afraid my uncle died in the explosion," he finished wistfully. He lay back, overcome with grief.

"Ye called for him in yir sickness."

The two men were silent for a while. Casey sat staring thoughtfully. "Sure'n there's somethin' dreadfully wrong here. For it's not a word I've heard from Sean since he left Ireland. Only once he wrote to say he had arrived and was ver-r-y sick." Casey rolled the "r" as if to emphasize the seriousness of Sean's illness. "He said he'd write to me when he made it to Indiana. He was plannin' to go as soon as he was well enough to travel. When I heard nothing, I wrote to George Brean meself."

Casey rose and took a worn carpetbag from its nail on the cabin wall. He pulled out a letter and handed it to Lee William. "This is from your uncle George. Yer story explains why this letter is saying what it says. When this came, I didna know what to do, so I made me way west and took a job here. I wanted to stay by the river so that when the war was over it'd be easier for me to travel . . . if I could get the nerve to go to Indiana. I didna think I'd be that welcome!"

Lee William looked at the paper, but the letters swam. He handed it back to Casey. "Please read it to me. My head's not clear."

Casey unfolded the paper and read the contents slowly.

Dear Mr. Brean,

Your letter of the 5th arrived. As you are a Brean, and therefore family to me and my dear sister, I wish you well in America. But I suggest that you will not want to come to Indiana making demands for your part of the farm, for you shall get none of it.

For three generations our family has dreamed of bringing the Irish Breans to America. When my sister's family moved to Missouri, I dared to hope that you and your brother might join me in farming the Brean family land. I was bold enough to imagine that the painting of Great-grandfather Brean would hang on the wall of this house that he built nearly a hundred years ago.

But now, I do not see that I can help you in any way. Nor can I help you in the matter of locating your brother. Sean Brean did come here and was with me for about six months. Then he disappeared one morning, taking with him a great deal of money that I gave him, but which he did not rightfully deserve. He also took my horse, which I did not give him. Furthermore, when I inquired about Great-grandfather Brean's painting, he did not know what I was talking about.

I can only assume that the Irish Breans did not keep their promise to preserve the painting until the last Brean from County Cork moved to America. It is quite

clear to me that it is not family, but money that concerns you. It is fortunate that my father did not live to see this turn of events.
George Brean

Lee William shook his head. "George was just steamed up, Casey. He thought you were coming to demand more money just like O'Reilly had done. But the last time I saw him, he knew that the man who'd come to the farm was an impostor."

"So he went after him to get his money?"

"I don't think he had hopes for recovering the money, at least not all of it. Mostly he wanted to clear up the mystery. Bringing you Breans to Indiana is his dream. He wanted to find out what happened to the real Sean Brean, and he was hoping to find you and explain . . . "

"He told you that?" Casey's face brightened.

"As the Almighty is my witness. He even said he would try to persuade you to come to Indiana."

Casey's delight was obvious, but soon his face clouded again. "I'm afraid for Sean. I know something must have happened to him."

Lee William nodded, for he knew Casey's pain as well. "We may never know now. I'm afraid both George and O'Reilly were killed on the *Sultana.*"

"Mebbe not, Lee William. B'gory, they pulled a lot of live ones out of the river. We had one crowded wood shanty that night. So many people standing around the stove—some had hardly enough clothes to cover them decent. But they were just glad to be alive."

Lee William brightened. "Maybe George was one of them."

Casey shook his head. "He wouldna have left ye here. No one knew ye. Ye were the only unconscious one. We put ye on that cot that ver-r-y night. Some of the ladies took care of ye. But no one knew yer name."

"Thank you, Casey." Lee William coughed harshly and then lay quiet.

"Ye're tired, ye are," said Casey. "I'll be leavin' ye so's ye can rest."

"I am tired, Casey. But I can't stay in bed forever. I've got to get home to my family."

"Soon . . . but ye must be stronger first. Now sleep."

Lee William closed his eyes and considered the ways of Almighty God. *I reckon God doesn't cause riverboats to blow up. On the other hand, He can take the bad things and bring something good out of them. If I hadn't been thrown off that riverboat, I wouldn't be here with Casey . . .* And Lee William slept peacefully, without visions of exploding boats and captains peering at him from amidst balls of fire.

CHAPTER TWENTY

Lee William's Return

❧

June, 1865

Lee William grew stronger daily. When a week had passed, he began to make plans to return home to Dogwood Creek. It took little convincing to persuade Casey to come with him.

Casey made the necessary arrangements. He bartered with his employer for a good riding horse and a stiff old white mare.

The morning they left, Casey took Great-great-grandfather Brean's painting down from the wall, wrapped it carefully in a clean shirt, and packed it in his carpetbag.

"I can't wait to see Mama's face when she sees that painting!" Lee William fingered a letter in his hand as he spoke.

"If ye're in mind to post that, we'll stop at the way landing upriver," suggested Casey.

Lee William nodded. "It's to the army headquarters in Cairo. I'm hoping they'll send my mustering out pay to me at Dogwood Creek."

––––––––––

They arrived at the landing within an hour. There, the two men heard the latest war news. The last Confederate forces had surrendered at Shreveport two weeks before. The rebellion was officially over.

After posting the letter, they mounted once more and quickly resumed their journey.

"I can't believe it, Casey," said Lee William. "It's finally over, really over. And I'm going home." Then, a bit later, "Won't Mama be surprised? I'm bringing home the last Brean from County Cork and—if the army answers my letter—I'll have enough money to pay off the farm!"

Casey looked at his newfound relative. "Sure'n, the only surprise that'll matter to her is having ye home."

Lee William's face grew serious. He shook his head and sighed.

"Would I be sayin' somethin' wrong, Lee William?" Casey asked.

"No, Casey," Lee William answered sadly. "It isn't you. I was just remembering how George was planning to visit Mama." His face grew grim, and his companion noted again the extreme fatigue and infirmity written on Lee William's face.

––––––––––

Lee William halted the roan horse on Solomon's Ridge beneath the great oak tree and drank in the scene below him.

He breathed deeply of the clean air—no stench, no vile vapors, just the pleasant odor of a sycamore-lined creek in mid-June.

Turning to Casey, he said, almost in a whisper, "So many times in Andersonville when I didn't think I could stand the smell another hour, I would shut my eyes and try to imagine this place. . . . I had to see it one more time."

Casey shifted nervously in his saddle atop the aging white mare and replied too quickly, "Sure'n there'll be years to enjoy it, Lee William—the rest of yer life."

"The rest of my life, yes. For I aim never to leave these hills again. But years? I reckon not. I've come home to die, Casey." He paused, coughing. "The best I hope for is to have time to arrange things for my family." He was silent for a moment and then, without looking at Casey, he asked, "Did I tell you about Little John?"

"Aye, ye did."

"He's the seventh child of the seventh son of the seventh child."

"B'gory—a special lad!"

"I've got to find a way to keep this farm free and clear." Lee William picked up his reins. "Enough about that. It's enough for today that I have lived to see Dogwood Creek again. Come, Casey," he called, "it's time you meet the rest of your family."

———

At the cabin below, MaryAnn rested from her gardening in the willow rocker on the front porch. Using the tail of her apron, she wiped the perspiration from her face and fought against the weariness that enveloped her. The cough

137

spasms had forced her to leave her work early, and she wondered as she rested how she could find the strength to go on.

If William John were alive, he would have told her, "Mary-Ann, you don't have to do it alone. Almighty God has not forgotten us yet." She smiled at the thought. Then she prayed aloud, "Almighty God, you have a mighty big job here with no menfolk to provide for these little ones, and us about to lose this dirt farm!" Sheepishly, she remembered that, at least for this season, God had brought both George and Russell to help. Smiling again, she admitted that God was God. He had not forgotten them yet.

"Who you talkin' to, Gramma MaryAnn?" Little John stood before her, water bucket in hand.

MaryAnn jerked up the tail of her apron and wiped her face again. "Never mind, Little John. Go on, fetch the water." As he disappeared down the path she called after him, "Mind the copperheads now."

A coughing spasm seized her. She clenched her fists and closed her eyes tightly, willing it to stop. "Almighty God," she prayed, half accusingly, "what is to become of Little John—of all of us?"

A horse whinnied from the direction of the ridge. MaryAnn rose from the rocker and walked around the corner of the cabin. She saw two riders approaching in the clearing above the barn. As they came closer she stared at the gaunt-looking rider hunched over a great roan horse.

Gasping to herself, she wondered, *Am I seeing a ghost? Is this really Lee William back from the dead?* She suppressed an impulse to meet the riders at the gate and went instead to call Lucy. "Come quick!" she called through the door. "Your man's come home from the war."

Little John, coming in at that very moment, dropped his bucket and ran headlong out the door. He was at the gate by the time his papa dismounted. He started to jump up into Lee William's arms as he had done many times before his papa had gone to the war. But Lee William squatted on his haunches and pulled the boy into his arms.

Choking back tears of relief and joy, he whispered, "Did you take good care of your mama, Son?"

Little John threw his arms around his papa's neck and burst into tears. "We thought you wuz dead, Papa! We thought you'd never come home agin!"

"Hush, Little John," commanded his sister Arial calmly. "You know Mama told you he'd be back. And Mama never lies."

Lee William rose carefully and kissed his daughters one at a time. Then he reached for Lucy, who stood silently waiting for his greeting. He clung to her, burying his face in her hair. Great sobs racked his emaciated frame. He kissed Lucy longingly. When he released her, he swept an arm toward Casey.

"Ever'body, this is our very own cousin from County Cork. Meet Casey Brean."

MaryAnn looked at the stranger, with his raven hair and beard. "No doubt in my mind," she declared. "You're a true Brean. You look like my Papa when he was young." She extended her hand.

Casey shook her hand warmly. "That would be cousin Michael Leland. I'm pleased to meet ye, ma'am. Lee William has talked of little else but his family."

Little John tugged at his mother's sleeve and begged to be allowed to fetch his uncle Russell from the field. She nodded. "Good idee, Son. And don't fergit Uncle George."

"George!" Lee William exclaimed. "George is here?"

Lucy smiled at her husband. "Sure is. He's workin' in the field with Russell."

"Casey, did you hear that? George is alive! He didn't die on the *Sultana* after all." Lee William threw his hat in the air. "Hallelujah! Do we have a surprise for him!"

CHAPTER TWENTY-ONE

Spring Comes to Dogwood Creek

───────── ❧ ─────────

Despite the excitement of the reunion, Lee William slept. Little John, having delivered the good news, ran all the way home from the field and spent the rest of the afternoon huddled in the corner of the bedroom, his eyes fixed on his sleeping papa. In the kitchen, MaryAnn and Lucy moved quietly about, preparing a supper fit for the occasion.

By the time Lee William awoke, George and Casey had become well acquainted, and Casey had agreed to go to Indiana with George at the end of the harvest season. A familiar voice called to Lee William from the doorway. "Hey, little brother, how about an arm wrestle?" He looked up to see Russell grinning at him. The two men embraced as Little John stood quietly by. Then the three huddled on the edge of the bed and talked until Lucy called them to supper.

At the table, the men heaped their plates with fried chicken and boiled potatoes, but Lee William refused to touch the cornbread.

"I'm sorry, Mama. I'm not sure I'll ever be able to eat anything made with cornmeal again!" He grimaced as he spoke. The pain in his eyes revealed how deeply Andersonville prison still haunted his memory.

As they ate, the family pieced together the events of the past six months. Lee William explained how he had found Casey. George repeated once again his account of Jake O'Reilly's death and Casey learned the truth about his brother.

"I'm sorry 'bout Sean," George said to Casey. "And I'm sorry 'bout the letter I wrote you. I should have known O'Reilly was an impostor."

"I would have known that man was not Sean Brean the moment he walked in the door," declared MaryAnn. "No red hair in this family!"

"It wasn't just his hair," said George. "Jake O'Reilly knew nothin' 'bout the family pictures. One day I showed him the place over the mantel where Great-grandmother's picture hung, and he didn't know what I was talkin' 'bout. It made me mad, thinkin' the Irish kin had lost the other paintin' years before Sean was born. I figured they didn't care much 'bout the family if they couldn't even care for Great-grandfather Brean's paintin'."

Casey scraped back his chair noisily and rose to his feet. He moved quickly toward the back door. When he reached for his carpetbag, George half rose and started to speak. Lee William stopped him, saying, "Don't worry, George. I think Casey has something to show ever'body."

Casey returned to the table with a bundle in his hand. Stopping before MaryAnn, he carefully unwrapped it for her to see.

142

MaryAnn gasped. "It's the other paintin'!" Speechless then, she reached for the picture, as tears ran slowly down her cheeks.

No one spoke until Lee William, unable to hold his excitement any longer, said, "Well, Mama, say something!"

"Yes, MaryAnn," George joined in, "say somethin'. Or are you just goin' to sit there dreamin' like you used to do over Great-grandmother Brean's picture?"

MaryAnn laughed through her tears. She laughed until the laughter dissolved into a coughing spell. Afterward, she admitted, "I reckon I did dream a lot in front of Great-grandmother's picture. Sometimes I was tryin' to imagine both paintin's hangin' together." Then, with a catch in her voice, she said to her brother, "Think of it, George, when you and Casey go to Indiana, Ian Brean's picture will hang on the wall of the house he built before we was born. I'm glad your dream's come true, George."

"That reminds me, Mama," said Lee William. "There's something I've been waiting to tell you. As near as I can figure, my furlough pay is just what we need to pay off the farm.

MaryAnn looked uncomprehending for a moment and then burst into tears. She hid her face in her apron until George broke the silence.

"I reckon that's good news, MaryAnn. 'Pears to me you ought to be laughin' instead of cryin'."

She raised her head, wiped her eyes, and smiled at George. "It's more than I had even prayed for." She glanced at the painting that now lay on the table. Turning to Casey, she suggested that he might like to hang Ian Brean's picture in the parlor until he and George left for Indiana.

Casey beamed his agreement. A few minutes later, all the family trooped into the parlor and watched as he hung the painting. When it was done, they broke into a great cheer. Clapping loudly, they stood back and gazed at the twin paintings hanging side by side.

MaryAnn shook her head wonderingly. "I can't believe it. So many dreams come true tonight." She walked to Russell's side and hooked her arm through his. "What about you, Son? You haven't said anythin' about your plans for quite a spell."

"We going to make a farmer out of you?" Lee William joined in.

"No chance, little brother. I got something else I got to do. Come fall, after crops are in, you'll not be needing me. So I'll just go back to St. Louis. Mr. Eads is fixing to build a bridge across the Mississippi and when he does, I want to be there."

He looked down at Little John and tousled his hair. Then, looking directly at Lee William, he said, "If you ever need me, I'll be here. But I expect by next planting season, you'll be fit as a fiddle. I'll leave the farming to you and Little John."

Little John tugged at his papa's arm. Then, speaking loudly so as to be heard above the din of voices, he asked, "Startin' tomorrow, kin I take care of your horse, Papa?"

The question puzzled Lee William, for he didn't own a horse. Then a look of understanding crossed his face. "You mean Casey's horse? The one I rode today?"

"Yes, Papa."

"As long as Casey's here, you can take care of that horse, Son. Suppose you tell me why you want to do that."

"Because, Papa. Because he brought you home from the dead."

A silence fell upon the room as every eye rested on the child. After a time, MaryAnn spoke.

144

"It was a fine spring day when we heard the war was over. But it didn't seem so to me. How could it be spring when my heart felt so much like winter? How could the war be over until our soldier came home?" She touched Lee William's shoulder gently. "Now, I reckon the war is finally over . . . spring has come at last."

"Yes, Mama," Lee William replied, looking at her with love and pride, "spring has finally come—for all of us."

Joy Pennock Gage was born in the Missouri Ozarks. She and her husband Ken spent five years in rural mission work, two of which were in a logging camp. They have ministered together in churches in California, Oregon, and Arizona. Joy is the author of numerous books, including *Is There Life After Johnny?* and *Every Woman's Privilege*. She currently lives in San Rafael, California. Joy's father, B.F. Pennock, *is* the seventh child of the seventh son of the seventh child, and she did have a great-grandmother named MaryAnn.